Wasted?

WASTED?

Hazel Edwards

Cover design by Joh Fitzpatrick
Typesetting by BookPOD

ISBN: 978-1-7635802-3-7 (pbk)
eISBN: 978-1-7635802-4-4 (e-book)

NATIONAL
LIBRARY
OF AUSTRALIA
A catalogue record for this
book is available from the
National Library of Australia

Contents

1. That Rubbish Idea 1

2. Garbage of Some Future Use 15

3. Lab Rats 35

4. Flashback: The Start-Up 45

5. Grace, Queen of Digital and the Lingo Ringo 51

6. Galley 67

7. Dragon Boat Mishap 79

8. The Great Garbo 97

9. Real Refugees 109

10. Changeover 119

11. Cal Consequences 133

12. Spy Cat 147

13. On Trial 179

14. What Happened to Wei Wei? 201

15. Ring Superpower 217

16. Palliative Care Hero 221

17. Expo: Refugee Legal Aid Cartoon Kit 231

    Acknowledgements 243

1

That Rubbish Idea

Was this the worst mistake he'd ever made? Joining a bunch of refugees in the middle of the ocean, next to the Great Garbage Patch? Leaving his dad in the hospital on the mainland? Forced to live again with his mum in ANOTHER community?

'Frederick?' Kit called out, positioning his canoe alongside the garbage raft on the landing side. The waves in the space between the two watercraft were choppy and the yucky water was murky with waste. Kit's paddle dipped into water with a texture like a yoghurt smoothie with crunchy bits. No way did he want to fall in there. Yet, so far out from the mainland, he was pleased he'd found the right place, first try: The Great Garbage Patch. And the satellite craft.

'Yeah!' Frederick replied.

Difficult to give yourself a high five in a canoe by yourself, but ... Kit did. He'd feared he'd be floating around for days. Plus he hadn't brought enough food and had eaten over half of it already. But he'd had to leave in a hurry. That was his excuse if anyone asked or if his stomach rumbled super loud.

'Come aboard, Kit. Your mum said you were joining us.'

'Why isn't she here now?' asked Kit, checking for her familiar face.

'Back soon. Off working.'

The dried out skin on the man's face and arms was weather-wrinkled like a smoked fish ... moisture sucked out of him. And on the sun-exposed leg muscles. Kit often drew people as animals or insects in his cartoon kit, and Frederick was definitely a smoked mackerel. Looming behind him was a recycled sort of houseboat with extra decks, solar panels, a satellite dish and green stuff growing in pots and tubs, which crept down the decks and softened the rough planks.

'Who'd want to live ... in the middle of the ocean ... on a garbage raft? Like a smelly prison,' Kit muttered. 'What's that noise? Is it a rocket?'

WHOOP WHOOP WHOOP.

They both looked up. Were they under attack?

'Look out. Bloody trauma tourists. Always wanting to gawk or demanding deliveries. That's a sling load. The chopper has a strong net underneath to carry stuff. Can even lift a canoe. Or useless luxuries for short-stay tourists.'

'Like what?'

'A hair straightener with extra batteries was one request. In case their hair got wet in ocean spray.' Frederick shrugged. 'We did suggest other things were more important out here.

2

Most expensive and useless delivery ever. But they paid for it, not us.'

'That looks like the harness used for Search and Rescue.' Kit watched the swaying load dangling from the cable, glad he wasn't directly underneath. Imagine if the chopper picked up him AND his canoe as a sling load. And dropped them in the sea, upside down. Gulping all that rubbishy water. No way.

'Look out. The supply chopper can't land on this deck – too small and crowded. So they sling-load stuff and drop it.' Frederick's voice was loud enough to hear clearly across the watery gap between Kit's canoe and the shantyboat.

Neatly, the helicopter dumped something on the crowded deck while a second chopper hovered like a shy but noisy twin egg beater.

'Cities are too loud. I've lived for years outside the legal limits, although sound travels on the water, as you would know,' shouted Frederick to prove it. 'And the choppers' noise is hard to miss.'

Disappointingly, the satellites Kit anticipated were just a fleet of second-hand sea craft, like mismatched houseboats circling the Great Garbage Patch. No rockets.

'Satisfying to build something from rejects, don't you think? Recycling is the future.' Frederick waited for a response.

Suddenly, Kit realised that if the choppers were built from rejects, that was another worry. Dad had told him about the metallic omelettes made when choppers crashed, with the bits recycled into a new flying machine for the next season. How many seasons had Frederick been here? And how many chopper bits had been recycled? Kit preferred his omelettes made from eggs.

'You could have refused Steffi's invite. All mums want to show off their kids. That's natural. Maybe Steffi sees you as another model youth for our satellite craft?' suggested Frederick.

'Mmm.' Kit kept Frederick talking. Too much water between them. And no choice. Kit was going to have to jump. He kept putting it off by chatting as his canoe moved up and down. 'Not me. Theo is ... like ... the model athlete on those refugee posters. Like, he won medals in the Olympics under the refugee flag. Then the TV *Survival* game. Like ... he's famous.' Theo's poster had been on Kit's bedroom wall in the old place.

'Have you met the Great Garbo? She's more your age.'

Kit shook his head. 'I know who she is ... AND a few months older than me. She won't be interested.' He was putting off making the leap on board, just in case ... Meanwhile, he sorted the mooring line.

He glanced down at the murky waste floating in the swirling tidal water between their vessels. Lots of plastic rejects here. And he knew sound travelled via water. Mum kept on about echolocation and her fish finding each other and themselves. No-one else had a mother into marine therapy who chatted

4

to her therapy dolphin in between dancing to the waves and the music of the spheres. Once he drew Mum as a butterfly, colourful and flapping, but she laughed and said she'd prefer to be a dolphin if he wanted to draw her soul. Steffi said that maybe SHE would draw HIM in return. But she didn't say which creature, and then she forgot about it. That happened a lot.

Kit eyed the deck. Could he jump that in one go? Or would he muck up and fall, as usual, because he knew Frederick's shrewd eyes were following his every move. No ladder. No rope. And all that yucky stuff.

He leapt.

'Aw!' Kit slipped on the wet deck. His knee went under him.

Frederick's sinewy arms grabbed him in time. 'You've made it! Well done, boy.'

So embarrassing. But at least he was on board.

Kit's ankles and knees didn't always do what his brain suggested. He rubbed his knee. Glancing sideways, he saw the mooring line had come undone all by itself and the canoe had started to float off with his backpack. He swore, and those words travelled across the water too. Not a good start to garbage patch living. Other vessels were secure in the mooring spaces: kayaks, canoes, zodiacs, known as rubber duckies (he knew that), and a few home-made punts. Crowded like a marina, but no millionaire yachts in sparkling blue and white. Just working hand-me-downs in need of paint, and with odd names. *X for Unknown* was the best. Others had girlfriend names like *Melania*. Or fish names like *Whale* or *Shark*. None called *Sardine*, like his canoe.

Kit's attention jumped back to Frederick, who in one smooth movement rescued the canoe and looped the mooring line securely. 'Try it this way next time.' He waved the chopper pilot goodbye.

'Thanks.' Kit didn't want a next time, ever. 'What if the chopper pilot misses with the drop? And it goes in the garbage?'

'She's pretty accurate most times. Choppers travel in twos for safety, you know. The other one is up there monitoring.'

'Yeah I noticed ... and heard.'

Glancing at the name label, Frederick moved the drop package to the side of the deck. 'I'll sort that later. Not an urgent delivery. Just one of Messi's schemes. Wei Wei was expecting urgent results via a drone, but ... this is not for her.'

Glancing at Kit's face, Frederick reassured, 'You'll get used to it. Wasted is a different kind of place to live, a mixture of recycled-old, which I prefer, and hi-tech.'

Kit was still confused.

Were you a proper country if you didn't have a wall or a border control post or a mountain range around you? What if anyone could send stuff online, use a drone or fly over? No borders. What made you a separate country? Was Wasted a new way of living, or just a dump? This wasn't outer space, it was outer ocean, but he had no choice. He'd have to give it a try. Mum had joined the Wasted community and hadn't given him other options.

'Yeah. I'll give you a hand if you like,' Frederick said.

Kit looked up. This garbage patch was more hi-tech than he expected. Choppers. Drones. 'So what does Chopper 2 do if something happens to Chopper 1? Can they pick up each other as a sling load?'

'Hasn't happened yet. There's a first time for everything. Chopper delivery is expensive out here. Like with Medivac, the tourists will be charged. Or their insurance will. Drones are cheaper. Mainly we email. We're a cashless society here. Or doing without is the cheapest. The simple life ... That's what I used to live.'

Tourists? Who'd want a holiday here? Kit didn't.

WHOOP WHOOP WHOOP. The second chopper circled and left.

'Welcome. There's a choice of tasks for you on board. "Pollucon", the Great Garbo calls it when she's interviewed. "Pollution conscription." Cleaning up. Re-using. D'you hear about the dumped sneakers? And how the Clean Oceans group digitally tracked who dumped stuff? Caught them. Your mum was talking about it on her Garbage Patch Podcast.'

Kit looked at his feet. 'Sort of ... Some idiot dumped lots of them in the ocean? And they're still there.' He didn't always listen to Mum online. She was always in a hurry, going nowhere. She called herself an eco-influencer but she didn't influence him, much. Steffi kept saying the same things. Boring as ... But he understood that Frederick thought he might be more interested in sneakers than ocean pollution.

'Anyways, I need another pair of hands to fix the new deck to give the lab rats more room.'

Rats on board, that's all Kit needed. Maybe he should leave now and paddle back home. But Dad wasn't there.

Should he draw the chopper sling-loading his canoe? Even if it never happened? Sketches were his way of hanging on to memories or possibilities. Usually Steffi 'lost' his artwork or binned it in the recycling. Dad always kept the latest cartoon framed on his bedroom wall.

'When Steffi said you were joining us, I made space for you. There's a sleep nook down there. And hooks and a hidden drawer underneath to store your stuff. You'll get used to living on the water.' Frederick automatically tidied a few ropes on the deck, coiling them neatly to create more space. He closed lockers, creating flat surfaces. And pulled the odd weed from the window plant boxes filled with tiny cherry tomatoes, which gave a splash of colour and looked fresh against the murky ocean. Like the green climber beans dangling down the deck.

'With a mum like mine, no choice.' Kit hauled up his backpack and dumped it on the deck under '*Satellite Freddie*', the name set in shells on the driftwood wall. So arty-crafty. Like Mum's woven stuff. He'd expected things to be more like Mars or outer space here. Satellite craft sounded like living on a rocket, or ... another planet. With scientists and way-out inventions. Not oldie art-and-craft stuff. Nor a vegetable garden on board with climbing beans taking over the world, and red cherry tomatoes like smiley faces!

Earlier he'd checked online. He knew satellite sea craft used as labs were grouped around the giant garbage patch formed by the ocean tides. But from this angle now, things looked more ordinary. Just distant dots on the ocean. Especially this houseboat raft. Disappointingly, not a rocket. He'd thought a raft was like just one plank. But this was a slightly moving flat deck at the first level, then different layers and modules, with leftover paint, mismatched texture walls on which were hooks, shelves and storage, and sort of cabins and balconies. Solar panels. A satellite dish like a crown on the top. How many lived here? Probably more than the moored share vessels indicated. Sharing ways of getting around. Like Mum, who was always getting lifts. Or trading favours. Steffi believed in the afterlife – lots of afterlives, depending upon which beliefs she was passionate about at that time. Steffi always claimed she wasn't a tourist expecting to be entertained; she was a traveller of cultures. Dad said she just liked running away.

～

A shadow fluttered across the deck. Kit looked up, just in time to see something dropping towards him from above. Like a giant rug or blanket, it floated down.

9

Kit dived sideways so he wasn't covered.

Sheet-like, the material wafted, fluttered and fell, covering the deck like a ghostly shape with ropes dangling. Kit struggled out of the ropes tangled with his leg.

A big man climbing above the top deck looked down and swore. In shorts, his thigh muscles looked super fit, tapering to strong ankles in functional navy deck shoes.

'Isn't that Theo the athlete, the one who carried the refugee flag in the Olympics?'

'Yes.'

'What is he doing?'

'Your guess is as good as mine. Probably trying to fix his flag on the mast. Or change it. Theo is always exercising his muscles in public.'

Against the light, it was hard to see the colours of the material or even work out if it was a flag, a sail or whatever.

As Frederick spoke, the big man stretched up, reached too far, and suddenly overbalanced and slipped. He fell, but quickly twisted in a somersault and landed on his feet on their deck. Those shoes had good grip. 'Circus acrobatics. Love aerial stuff.' His voice was pleasantly deep with an accent Kit couldn't place. Annoyingly, he wasn't even out of breath. Kit was so impressed Theo could land on his feet on a moving deck.

'Hi. Did you see that twist?' Theo asked.

Kit nodded.

Frederick shrugged. 'Waste of time showing off. Dot, the female chopper pilot, has gone.' And he was already folding up the fallen material. Frederick liked a tidy deck, no question about that. Kit realised then what the material was. A flag. Orange and black.

Theo nodded. 'Meant to be coloured like the safety life jackets of the refugees fleeing on dodgy smugglers' boats. But officials changed the maritime rules, so not sure about whether the refugee flag can be used now.'

Theo turned to Frederick.

'I was having a bit of a look around. Frederick, have you noticed anything unusual being carried this way by the currents?'

'Take your pick. The Great Garbage Patch is full of stuff brought by the currents.'

'No sneakers yet? Or odd packages?'

'Only bloody tourists bringing the gift of Covid. And Cal was the one who got it. Are you vaxxed, Kit?'

'Yes. Triple. My dad made sure.'

Theo coiled the ropes that had fallen with the flag. Kit would have helped but didn't know what to do without getting in the way. He didn't want to trip over the tub of yellow and red chillies or damage the creepers of greenery. With his luck, he probably would. Safer to stand still.

'Has anyone designed a special Wasted flag yet? Want one? Happy to do it. I like designing things.' Kit had learnt from Steffi: best to volunteer for something you liked doing, before you got one of the yucky jobs.

'Too many regulations about flags. If we can't use the refugee one here, no hope of using a Wasted one.' Theo picked up the folded sheet-like material. 'Have work to do below. See you later.' Theo left, taking his energy with him.

Frederick shrugged. 'Got to sort out what are the most important things to do first on board this shantyboat.'

'Like what?'

'Clean drinking water. Building stuff. Something to trade. Watching football finals by satellite?'

Both laughed.

Not good at judging ages, Kit decided Frederick was vintage ocean. This weather-wrinkly man with 'Frederick' tattooed on his sinewy arm would be a challenge to draw.

'You're pretty old. Sorry. Was that like, rude?'

'Yeah. But age is a fact. Like distance. Or ocean depth. Or measurements. Inside, some of us feel different from outside. Like your mum, Steffi. How old are you?'

'Seventeen soon.'

'How soon?'

'End of next year.'

'Can't remember much about being your age 'cept for playing LEGO and building Meccano.'

Frederick was so last century. Kit knew about LEGO but not the other stuff.

'Aren't you scared of getting older stuck so far out here? And dying?'

'Nah. Don't work like I'm 20 any more. I just allow a bit longer. More worried about the planet's future than my own. And if I'm dead, I won't know what's happening anyways.'

'Will you have a sea burial?'

Frederick looked directly at Kit to see if he was serious. 'Not yet. Got a few things to build this week. Wasn't considering a biodegradable coffin yet. When the time comes, your mum would probably paint dolphins all over it. But I won't have to worry about that.'

He smiled. Then Kit let out a grin too.

For a water weirdo, Frederick might be okay. Maybe they could get on? Easier than avoiding the Great Garbo, who was on board. A 16-year-old Head of State who probably wouldn't talk to him much. Only a few months difference, but ... head-spaces apart. She was internationally famous, always on the climate news as a conscience reminding adults that youth needed a clean future. He was just Steffi's embarrassing son who needed a home.

'Theo was on the *Survival* show. I saw him win,' Kit said. 'Watched every episode.'

Frederick looked up. 'So did I. And he got pretty mad at one of the other contestants who kept putting down refugees and asylum seekers. Some racist "put-downs" with bad taste jokes.'

Kit hadn't heard that.

'What was the bad taste joke?'

'It wasn't broadcast. The TV director switched to a commercial.'

'Oh. Is that censorship?'

'If you really want to know, ask Theo,' suggested Frederick. 'I don't like repeating stupid stuff. Theo stood up to them. He called them out on national TV. Told them off. That's why I can put up with his carrying-on now.' Then Frederick added, 'Theo's a good bloke to have on board. He's got no sense of smell. That helps around here.'

A black cat with a studded collar padded across the deck, circled Kit and kept going down the stairs.

'Shadow's come to meet you. Always inspects visitors.'

Kit wasn't a cat person. He preferred drawing creatures, not patting them.

'If a black cat crosses your path, some believe that's good luck.' Frederick smiled.

'Or is it bad luck? My mum Steffi thinks cats are shapeshifters moving between worlds.'

'Just superstition. No proof either way.'

'So why did the cat cross my path?'

'On the way back to the lab. That's just Shadow, the ship's cat. She's adopted Wei Wei, our Chief Seeker, who does all the science stuff. But Wei Wei hasn't adopted her.'

Kit had noticed the tiny body-cam on the cat's collar. Who put that there? And why?

2

Garbage of Some Future Use

'What do you think of all this?' Frederick indicated the boat and the garbage patch beyond. A haze of grey-blue bobbing along the horizon. 'All the vessels are a bit different. More are joining us.'

Kit shrugged. It didn't smell much at the moment, just looked messy, as if the ocean couldn't clean itself. Reminded him of the time Dad took him camping in the bush, and he asked why the trees didn't sweep up their own messy leaves. Must have been about 4 then. Dad had laughed.

'Thought it would be like living on Treasure Island and finding stuff ... you know, like trash and treasure markets or op shops, but ... are the others all asylum seekers? Or refugees? Were you?'

'Nah, I'm a tradie ... Love fixer-uppers. That's what this garbage raft is, a giant fixer-upper. A love job at "mates' rates". They need a few basic building skills as well as scientific geniuses. Most are refugees trying to earn a visa. Hard workers. And then the asylum seekers often have different reasons for being here.'

'Mum says the seekers are making recycled treasure from trash here ...'

'They're clever all right. Like a climate change repair shop, that's how I'd describe this place. Bio-stuff. Most disagreed with the powers-that-be in their own countries. Or got caught in war zones. Had to leave their homes to save their families ... or else! Then got stuck in refugee camps and couldn't get visas to go anywhere. Like Dr Wei Wei. Now she's experimenting with garbage here to fix stuff. Others call it trash.'

'What did you do before?'

'A chippie.'

'Sold fish and chips?'

'Nah. A chippie is a carpenter.'

Kit went red. He could feel the flush growing over his face. So embarrassing. He was sick of getting things wrong. Maybe he could grow a beard soon and cover embarrassing blushes, then no-one would know how much he didn't know.

'Used to have an off-grid bush hut before I moved on the water,' Frederick continued.

'Is it better living on the water?'

'Yeah. In my bushie, I had a dirt floor and water came in buckets from the creek. Lighting was from candles and kerosene lamps. Here solar pumps are a step up.'

Kit looked at the hi-tech solar panels and satellite dish positioned between the re-used wood, miscellaneous paint colours and sprouting pot plants in odd containers. This was definitely a work-in-progress boat.

Frederick watched, realising Kit didn't know what to say. 'Never get the beautiful boat award, but it all works.'

'You reckon people will WANT to live here?'

'If you're being threatened, you'd settle for this for a little while.'

'Threatened? Anyone threaten you?'

Frederick raised an eyebrow, then became very busy moving stuff.

Kit shrugged. 'Okay. By threats, did you mean bullying? My dad has had some of that. When you lived off-grid, what was different?'

'Harder work. Started life in a corrugated iron shed. Then we moved into a compressed earth house. My pump was hooked up to a makeshift machine for fuel. I was an off-grid groundbreaker.' He laughed.

'Who was "we"?'

'You ask too many questions.'

'M'dad used to say that was the only way to learn. Ask the right questions.'

'That wasn't one of them.'

Kit knew Frederick noticed he said 'used to' ... about Dad. Frederick would know who Dad was and where he might be. Was that going to be a problem? Had Steffi talked much on board about Dad's discoveries? And how his ideas were attacked? The threats for him to keep quiet. Or only about her marine therapy?

'Sorry.'

'Going on scavenger hunts, that was our day out. At a scrap yard I bought solar panels for a dollar a kilo. Spent my nights on YouTube picking up tips from others living this way ... or off-grid. And then I moved out here ... all water ... At night, watch the footy on my solar-powered satellite TV.' Frederick sounded more cheerful when he talked about footy.

'Do you call that being self-sufficient?'

'No. But I like doing it. Who do you barrack for?'

'Whoever I'm talking to – their team. Yours if you like.' Kit shrugged. 'Tell me about your early days here. You know, like, back in ancient history.'

Frederick focused on Kit.

'Raft 1 was my demo. A few seekers seem to have forgotten that. Sort of grafted their ideas onto mine. A bit like mudbricks: you keep on adding rooms or gardens or adapting stuff. Not that we're short of stuff from the garbage dump. Just got to work out how best to use it.'

'What do you do if you don't know how to fix stuff?'

'Find a YouTube clip. Or google: "How to fix ...?"' Frederick winked. 'I learnt to read words like "bioremediation" pretty fast.'

'That's two words, isn't it?' Kit wasn't sure. When you didn't know a language, or scientific labels, several run-together sounds were like one word.

'That's the BIG word around here. The seekers are working on that.'

'Yeah.'

'You learn new swear words around here pretty quickly too, even in a few dialects. Bolour's the official translator, or used to be before they invented this Lingo Ringo gadget.'

'I've used XChange once. Do you speak many languages?' Kit couldn't think of a language old enough. 'Like Latin?'

'Nah. Use the Lingo Ringo app. It's better than the old XChange. Don't have to learn new languages to understand newcomers if a gadget does it for you. Frederick indicated his ring and the sunlight glinted on it. His fingers were like dried mackerel-skin sausages.

'Grace invented the ring so refugees could understand each other quickly, without a translator. Even those who don't read in their own language. Got a patent and we traded the idea. Others pay to use it. Wasted gets the money. That's what keeps us afloat.'

'Afloat. Ha! Got that!' Kit suspected Frederick had used 'afloat' before. He recycled more than boat parts. He played with words too. A bit like Dad.

Frederick checked the local time on his digital ring. Sunlight flickered, making the colours alive like a rainbow.

'Does that work in different time zones?'

'Of course. Grace, our Queen of Digital, built in lots of useful stuff ... Can't work out half of it.'

'If you're crossing the International Date Line, does it still work?'

'Good question. Never tried. Didn't have the ring when I sailed around the world. Grace hadn't invented it then. Didn't even know her. Now, we anchor around the garbage patch mainly. Probably would work.'

'Once, my dad flew across the International Date Line on his birthday and said he had two birthdays.'

Frederick nodded. 'Lucky he wasn't going the other way. The workers will be back soon from their salvaging trips. One shift is still sleeping, so we'll need to be quiet. Like oil rigs or mines. Always someone working. Or using the equipment.'

Kit glanced back to check *Sardine* was still attached. That was his escape route if *Satellite Freddie* raft turned into a prison. As long as no-one else borrowed the canoe first.

'Awesome job, this raft, Frederick. Did things ever go wrong back in the olden days of this boat ... sorry ... when you started around the garbage patch?'

The deep wrinkles on Frederick's dried face moved into different patterns when he smiled. Watching closely, Kit knew how he could draw Frederick's lips. Like a cartoon creature. With thick lip-filler. And uneven teeth behind. But kind eyes.

'Want to draw me, Kit?'

'Later.'

Could Frederick read his mind? Nah. Not possible. Sometimes, Kit surprised even himself with what he found inside his own head. How could anyone outside work it out?

'What went wrong? That's what they all ask,' Frederick replied. 'We almost sank. Decks fell in the garbage. The water desalination didn't always work. A few worried about possible smells. Not Theo.'

'Biggest problem?'

'Generator breaking down. Anchor floated off. Lab cupboards up so high Wei Wei couldn't reach. She's seriously short. Sleep nook hooks that collapsed in the night. Leaks in the hold. But people who argued were the worst. Fixing things was easier than fixing people.'

'Is that what you did?'

'Still trying. Too many threats. Weather. Politicians who want credit for things they didn't invent. Because so many vulnerable refugees need a place, we're just making a model here first. Like a pilot scheme. With a small number of people. If it works here, others can make their own versions.'

Kit wasn't sure how to respond.

'You can tie your shoelaces, can't you?' Frederick challenged Kit.

Then Frederick looked at Kit's feet and they both laughed.

'Okay. No laces. But I'll show you a square knot and see if you can copy me.'

Frederick threw two ropes at Kit, then got busy knotting his own two ropes. 'This is a square knot. It joins two rope supports.' His strong, stubby fingers moved so fast. He warned Kit, 'If you get it wrong, you'll end up with a granny knot and that comes undone too easily.'

With his two ropes, Kit imitated the knotting sequence of Frederick's fingers. He looked up for the older man's reaction.

'Looks like rough knitting' – Frederick examined the knot – 'but good job for a first effort.'

Kit admitted, 'Dad taught me that one. But I wouldn't mind learning the others.'

'Fair enough,' Frederick said. 'Seafarers and mountain climbers depend on knots. Some knots are known by different names.'

'I thought a knot was mainly about how fast the boat travels.'

'That too. But we're not moving anywhere at present.'

Remembering getting seasick a while ago, Kit asked anxiously, 'Will the rafts move ... like, with the tides and wind? Or are they anchored to the sea floor? What about when the tides get ... sort of ... really rough? Like ... in a bad storm?'

Frederick nodded. 'With oil platforms you can keep adding modules. They're anchored and use traditional materials. Not sure about modules based on trash. That's what we're playing around with now ... how to add on bits to make fake islands. But consistency of trash is a problem.'

'So the boat's a work in progress?'

'Yeah. Plenty of supplies.' Frederick gestured towards the garbage patch.

'Anything else you can use?' Kit decided it was better to know how he might drown before it happened. Knowing about knots mightn't be enough to save him.

'A floating base of any sort – ship hull, empty fuel tanks, lightweight concrete. The Chinese have played around with floating islands as military airfields.'

'Like in floating jetties?'

'Yeah ... could be expanded using rubbish.'

Seems like Frederick knew his stuff. But Kit didn't know if he could survive here. What if he were stuck on this raft world until he looked like Dried Fish Man? Mum's mad ideas, like mind-body fitness with auras, usually lasted for months. But if living with Dad wasn't an option, where could he go? If he still had the canoe, he could leave. Go where? Nowhere was home any more.

Frederick spoke up. 'Get a ring from Grace, our Digital Queen, and sign up for shifts. Be careful climbing up or down to the next deck. Don't want to break anything. Or wreck my creepers by grabbing on to them.'

'Okay. I'll check on the different knots too.'

Kit went below slowly, one step at a time, his knee twinging a bit, to check out his new home. The boat did move quite a bit already. Where was Grace? He'd find her. *Satellite Freddie* wasn't that big. Just had to sort out the levels.

⌐

A kayak arrived and a figure scrambled aboard. Steffi dropped some sleeping bags in front of Frederick, who was clearing the deck.

'More of your stuff, Steffi?'

'Like them?'

Frederick shrugged. 'Depends how you want to use them. By the way, your son Kit turned up. That's his canoe attached there.'

'I recognise the *Sardine*. Used to belong to my ex-husband.'

'Kit's down below sorting his space. Give him a chance to explore on his own. Like an adventure. Back up in a minute.'

'I hadn't forgotten he was coming.' Steffi was always quick with excuses about why she was somewhere else. 'I just had to visit the other shantyboats with the trauma tourists. They paid to shadow me for a day. Sold them some stuff. Explained about the pollucon credits for visas. They didn't seem keen to try. Just took selfies.'

'I told Kit to get a ring from Grace. And find out which shift he'd be working on the garbage patch.'

'Thanks, I'll find him.' Steffi flicked back her long, multi-streaked hair. Her patchwork vest was embroidered neatly with leftover materials. Sensible shoes for deck work. Steffi was an odd combination of practical and other-worldly. An aqua silk veil was stuffed in one bag and the end fluttered as if it wanted to escape.

'Was going to weave Kit a new sleeping bag from recycled stuff but had a few interruptions. What did you think of the snooze-bags I made for the others?' Steffi offered the bags. 'Choose one for yourself. Thought you might like the rope one. Knots, like you showed me.'

'Memorable.' Frederick always said 'memorable' when he was struggling for words. Covered both good and bad situations. The unexpected thing was that Steffi's craft work was beautiful but she needed to be praised, frequently. Her knitting and weaving were intricate, and she used whatever could be recycled. Even marine rope for knitting. Her knots were even and well positioned.

Frederick wasn't so keen on the *'Satellite Freddie'* spelled in shells and glass fragments, but upsetting Steffi meant she was moody for ages. Better just to ignore it. He tried not to look at the *'Satellite Freddie'* sign. Only his ex-partner used to call him Freddie.

Steffi had talked her way over here from Refugee Camp 13 with Wei Wei and Bolour. But Frederick was unsure if recycled snooze-bags with artistic knots were a top priority. As a carpenter he appreciated the beauty of a well-designed piece of art, but did they have time for Steffi's arty stuff on board? Too many refugees dying on dodgy boats run by people smugglers. And if they survived the ocean, even when they got to the camps there was nowhere else to live. He sighed and turned back to Steffi.

'Designed anything new that might help now? Could be copied quickly?'

Steffi nodded. 'Cal did. That fold-up mini-tent, in the side-pack made from recycled trash. I just helped, but it was her idea and she should get the credit. Mentioned it on my podcast and got such good feedback. It's a Wasted tent. Could be used in the temporary camps. Or in flooded areas. Or after bushfires. While governments are stuffing around with emergency equipment, which doesn't arrive or gets stolen or sold on the black market.'

'Maybe.' Frederick wondered if the refugees who needed temporary tents listened to Steffi's podcasts. Or the officials? Unlikely.

'Let me show you.'

Steffi opened the tent-within-a-bag. 'No zips. Just press clips. Warm. Pockets. Shoulder strap. Waterproof. Murky colours. Safety light. Warning device. Can float. Use as a sleeping cape.'

'Practical.' Frederick was unexpectedly impressed. Steffi's ideas were often unworkable.

'Cal sanitised it first with that eucalyptus stuff. I taught her to sew the heavier material.'

'Are they going to patent the design?'

'No. Giving it away for free.'

'Like the Covid vaccines.'

'Yes. Cal and I agreed on that. Quick use by more refugees, rather than involving lawyers. Especially Lex, who always wants his cut for chargeable minutes.'

Frederick had never met Lex, but knew who he was: Wasted's legal person who knew EVERYTHING about patents and 'who got what' when ideas were licensed. He never even visited the garbage patch. But Wei Wei said that without Lex, Wasted was not protected. They needed his skills to trade and form their state. Maybe Wei Wei was right?

But Frederick wasn't impressed by an international lawyer who couldn't make time to visit in person. Lex didn't understand what they were trying to do. Refugees were just numbers to him.

Frederick was surprised at Steffi's decision. 'Free is good. Will you call it the Cal tent? Or the Steffi?'

What Steffi said and what she eventually did wasn't always the same. Maybe Cal had influenced her this time?

Steffi shrugged. 'Doesn't matter. I'll talk about it again on my podcast anyway.'

'Any news about Cal's health?'

'No ... Complications after Covid and the antibiotics for an infection, Wei Wei said. Waiting on more test results from the mainland.'

'Okay, time for me to work below. I'll send Kit up to you.'

Frederick vanished, feeling unexpectedly cheered by Steffi's rare, usable effort.

~

'Hi Mum.' Kit's head appeared from below, then he stepped onto the deck, gave his mum a hug and fingered the sleeping bags. 'Is this your latest project?'

'I told Frederick to look out for you. He's a kind soul from a previous life.'

'I've met him.'

Frederick was kind, but like everybody on board, seemed to have secrets from his previous life. Kit had mixed feelings about seeing his mum. He knew not to ask her where she'd been. Rangi, God of the Sky, the Māori bloke, was her latest relationship, and Kit hadn't met him, but Dad was always his dad.

Before Kit came, he'd imagined these satellite boats were a bit like ocean prisons in their own space. A mixture of hand-me-down trash. However, people seemed to move around between them and even go to the mainland to restock food and supplies. They weren't totally isolated.

Steffi had visited Dad several times on the mainland during her resupply trips. Kit knew that, even though he hadn't always known his mum was coming.

'One of my jobs is organising food supplies from the

mainland for all the satellites,' said Steffi. 'Want to have a look at where we store things? I knew food would interest you.'

'Okay.'

'Follow me. But let's put these away first.'

Kit helped bundle the Cal tents into one of the lockers on the deck. He'd prefer sleeping in the Cal tent on the deck rather than the sleep nook beneath, but ...

Hard to tell how many lived on board, as the sleeping bags and hammocks were in the hidden storage walls or under benches. A stray foot poked out. And the odd snore. Strangers smiled and squeezed past in the narrow passageways. All ages. And shapes. A few accents.

'Hi.'

'How's it going? Who's the new lad?'

'Heard the chopper. Did it bring what those tourists ordered?'

'Any news of Cal?'

Steffi introduced everybody but after a while the names blurred, so Kit just nodded. Every bit of space was used for more than one purpose. Seats lifted up and revealed tightly stacked lockers beneath. Clever. Doors moved to reveal secret cupboards.

Frederick's face appeared around a corner. 'Let me show you my handiwork. I'm a bit proud of my tiny carpentry in small spaces. So we can fit in more people.'

'Catch up with you soon,' said Steffi.

Kit followed Frederick and looked on in admiration as he pulled down hammocks or unfolded extension tables that were also backs of something else. Like a wooden jigsaw puzzle. Each piece fitted perfectly, as Frederick pointed out – a few times.

'Here's the head, or the bog or the loo … Different names for this, but it's the compost toilet.'

Yuck. At least it wasn't just hanging off the end of the raft.

'We have hot-bed spaces in the sleeping quarters.'

'Heating?'

Frederick smiled. 'Like hot desks, take it in turns? And there's a compact shower too. Hoses for wastewater.'

Kit praised the recycled tubs in tiny spaces. 'Herb gardens in barrels? I thought the tiny cherry tomatoes looked … er … colourful.'

'Edible too.' Frederick nodded. 'Zucchinis, peppers and beans. Mushrooms down below in the dark spaces.'

'No sweet stuff or …'

'Strawberries. Raspberries too, but they're not such good growers here.'

A thick-set stranger stood sideways to let them through. His chunky chest muscles took up almost the width of the passageway. Clambering space only.

'Meet Mohammed.'

'Hi Mohammed. I'm Kit.'

Kit dithered and then lunged left, unsure about whether

it was legal or polite to pass left or right. And whether he'd even fit.

Mohammed waited. Then he nodded and moved through, sideways.

'On board, who has right of way? Left- or right-hand side?' Kit asked.

'Law of the Sea is only for vessels, not people,' Frederick explained. 'Powered vessels must turn to starboard ...'

'That's right'

'... pass at a safe distance. On board, people just need to be polite.'

'Got it. Pleased to meet you, Mohammed,' said Kit, turning back, but the big man had gone, squeezing through sideways like a giant crab. This crab-like man had excellent manners for the Law of the Sea. Maybe he should draw Mohammed later.

'In the olden days, cannons could only fire 12 nautical miles from the mainland. So that's how far Law of the Sea applies.'

'Can't see any cannons here. Or guns. Or police. Or soldiers.'

Frederick laughed. 'We're aiming for a no-crime, perfect society. Utopia. Our Wasted State claims 12 miles on any side. But if Wasted adds extra islands and atolls, we can claim more ocean space, legally. Like those fake islands in the China Sea.'

'So we're copying illegal takeovers?' Kit watched the TV news with Dad most nights at home.

'No, we're creating a state for homeless refugees. Giving them legal status. That's different.'

'Says who?'

Frederick didn't respond. Maybe he hadn't heard. Or maybe he was sick of talking about refugees. 'Selective deafness' Steffi called it when Kit pretended not to hear stuff.

The next cabin had lots of navigation and other equipment. Lights, dials, gauges and screens. Like a mini control room with charging stations and storage lockers.

'Our internet connections are good. And we have enough battery storage for three months if the weather turns bad and there's no solar power. We mounted some extra solar panels on the steel rail and these can slide out and provide shade too.'

'What if it's not sunny?' Kit was learning that Frederick heard technical questions perfectly, but not always ones about people.

'We have a generator for cloudy days when the solar can't keep up. We carry foul weather gear just in case.'

'Do you stay beside the garbage patch mainly or do you go back to the mainland?' Kit fiddled with the shiny panel of buttons, trying to work out which control did what.

'Hey, leave that, Kit,' Frederick cautioned. 'We're staying put around here. The smaller craft go to the mainland, but only for essentials.'

'Like food?' Kit asked. 'The stuff you don't grow?'

Frederick nodded.

'The instruments can be put on autopilot, but we're not like most motor-sailors. We tend to hang around the Great

Garbage Patch and don't travel the world's oceans. Well, not yet anyway. Most off-grid boats are owned by adventurers who want to follow the seasons or circle the world. Been there, done that. Happy to hang around here and help Wei Wei's projects. We've got a reliable anchor now; had to replace the earlier one. That's important if you want to stay in the one place for a bit.'

'Within 12 miles of the garbage patch?'

'Got it. Nautical miles. Yes. Our original dinghy was like our "truck" for transportation, but now all these other vessels have joined us. And we share –'

'Can I recharge my device later?'

'Sure.'

Kit didn't want to lose his sketches. He also wanted to feel that he was still in touch with the outside world, and maybe Dad, if necessary.

Steffi joined them. 'Need to check on the "Clean Oceans" campaign.' She fiddled with the screens. 'Oh no. Not more bad news.'

Text ran across the screen.

'The Space Centre's rocket has crashed,' Steffi said. 'Debris still falling over a wide area. Some may fall in the ocean. There will be closer surveillance of all the waste in the various currents.' Steffi looked at the screen, which was showing a map, and then left quickly.

'Messi won't be happy about more surveillance of the

currents round here. Or surveillance of the other islands. Or anyone checking on him and his schemes.'

Kit didn't realise the significance of what was happening. Or who Messi was. Kit was just a kid living on a reclaimed garbage raft. Soon he would be part of history.

～

3

Lab Rats

'Come and meet Wei Wei's lab rats.'

For a moment, Kit imagined real rats. With whiskers and running over him. Yuck.

It was as if Frederick read his mind. 'Lab rats are seekers working on the recycling project. People, not actual rats. Used to be social justice activists. Wei Wei is so keen, she converted them to climate change.'

'Yeah. I guessed that.'

'This is the plastics laboratory. Luckily Wei Wei's tiny, so she doesn't mind having a tiny lab.'

Kit peered through the open doorway. The Chief Seeker was a petite woman who was probably as old as his mum. Hard to tell. There were a couple of assistants squeezing around her who nodded 'Hi' to Kit and kept comparing results. Both were short, slim and moved deftly. Each had on safety goggles that made them look like bugs.

On a tiny bench were tubes and liquids for testing, super organised by colours and shapes, plus chemistry equipment

Kit didn't recognise. Buckets with lids under the benches. For a moment, Kit wondered if Wei Wei was blind. No. Just economical with her movements, quickly feeling for things. No way could he live or work with her in this confined space. Made him feel claustro– … whatever that word was. The King of Clumsy, he would drop or break the tubes in five minutes. Knotting that rope had been a real achievement for him, but his dad was keen on practising stuff until you got it right.

'Yeah, getting a bit crowded. No quota on our shantyboats 'cos it sounds too much like visa quotas.' Frederick squeezed into the tiny lab. 'And the asylum seekers are fed up with official forms that go nowhere. So I just build another landing or annexe. Need to keep the raft balanced. That keeps me busy.'

The two lab-rat assistants were sort of moving to music through their earbuds. Each wore protective gloves, with a bump which must be a Digital Lingo Ringo.

'Wei Wei, this is Kit, Steffi's lad.'

Wei Wei gave a fleeting smile but when she took off her goggles, her eyes were somewhere else. Her black hair was twisted and pinned in a casual ponytail with tufts escaping. Tiny grey-silver streaks shone against the black hair.

'Did you arrive by canoe, Kit?'

He nodded. '*Sardine*. That's the name of my canoe.'

'Maybe ocean-walking on water will be possible soon for anyone, with a bit of help from recycled mini jet-skis.'

'Wow.' Kit imagined drawing that.

'All good. Since our refugees have repurposed themselves as science activists, anything is possible.'

For such a tiny person, confident Wei Wei had a big, clear voice, except she swallowed the ends of her words. She was very formal, as if talking to a camera.

'Our opportunity to create a perfect nation. All will benefit from trading our bioremediation ideas.'

More big words, thought Kit. But it's just marine debris, ropes and all that plastic. Watery junk.

Was this the moment to mention the rocket debris to show he knew something about types of recent trash in the ocean? No.

But Frederick thought otherwise. 'Heard the news about the rocket crash?'

Wei Wei looked up. 'Again? I've been concentrating on cleaning up Earth, not littering outer space.'

That was a surprise. Kit imagined she'd be interested in any scientific news.

'When's Cal back?' asked Frederick. 'Having more tests?'

One of the lab rats explained, 'Soon, I hope. I've been doing her job for a while now. The trauma tourists gave us the gift of Covid, brought it with them. Poor Cal was the only one who caught it.'

Wei Wei said, 'I worry about her too. She had anti-virals, then we organised antibiotics for the infection in her arm, but we thought we'd better do another test as well. Just waiting on the results.'

'So we're being extra careful about contamination.' The dark-haired lab rat held up his gloved hands and adjusted his mask.

The other lab rat, with the fashionably shaved head, said, 'Cal was off for a few weeks with Covid and then, when she came back, she broke her arm falling down the stairs from the upper deck.'

Sounds like Cal was a bit clumsy too. That was a relief.

'Meet Shadow.'

Suddenly, the black cat with the unusual studded collar coiled its way around the shelves. Like most cats, it acted as though it owned even this tiny space.

'Shadow is welcoming you to her place.'

Kit doubted that. Cats made him sneeze.

'ACHOO!'

Frederick patted the cat, but Kit jumped aside and bumped his head on the low roof.

'And also meet Shadow's very new family. We've just found them in the lab shelf behind the cupboard. That was a surprise.' Lab Rat 1 pointed to black kittens. As someone so precise, how did Wei Wei cope with new kittens?

She didn't.

'Lab rats! Deal with the kittens.' The assistants moved quickly. 'And move that kitty litter out. Don't need a cat toilet in here.' Lab Rat 2, the bald one, took out the brown crumbles on the tray.

Wei Wei half-turned to Frederick but kept checking results.

'Done anything about my lift idea for other craft, Frederick?' she asked him.

'Short answer: no.'

'Lift-off?' Kit imagined a rocket while trying to take up as little space as possible with his physical body.

'Lifts have a passenger and weight limit when weight and occupied space would make more sense.'

'Yeah. Seen that sign in high-rise lifts on the mainland.' Kit nodded. 'Limit: nine passengers.'

'Equipment weighs more than people,' Frederick commented. 'Could simplify. Off-load some of our junk from the shantyboats? But building a lift takes up too much space.'

'Our satellite rafts should limit people by combined weight and brain power. AND I suggested a clumsiness ratio. You wouldn't pass,' said Wei Wei as Kit tripped, crashed into the bench and swept all the test tubes onto the floor when his hand grabbed the nearest ledge.

He tried to put things back, apologising. 'Sorry, so sorry.'

'That's our morning's work wasted.' Wei Wei looked at his hand and sighed. 'You're bleeding. Here. I'll clean you up.'

She rummaged in a cupboard neatly built underneath the tiny table. Probably Frederick's work, with an F signature finely carved in the polished wooden corner.

'Can't save the world if I have to clean up people like you all the time.' Neatly, Wei Wei disinfected the wound and covered it. Very practised, as if she'd done it millions of times.

'Are you ... like ... a doctor?'

'Used to be. In another life. Before things went wrong. And freedom fighters became rebels.'

'Thank you ... er ... Dr Wei Wei.'

Kit knew about Camp 13 activists. Mum had been there too, as a refugee after she lost her ID papers in the uprising and couldn't cross the borders. When Steffi had mentioned a camp doctor, Kit assumed the doctor was male. That doctor was blamed for a risky operation on ex-Prince someone-or-other. It had gone tragically wrong. And the rebels blamed the doctor. But with Steffi it was hard to tell how much she exaggerated stories to make life more interesting. And Steffi would be cross with Kit for thinking the doctor had to be male.

Sounded as if Wei Wei might have been the doctor. And a freedom fighter? Or a rebel?

Kit tried to help in the lab but wasn't sure where to put things. Wei Wei placed a first aid box with a red cross on the bench in front of him. *CRASH!* The cat landed on the box, claws scrabbling. Again Kit noticed the tiny digital camera attached to its collar as he firmly pushed the cat away. Was Kit being cam-recorded? Why? Who would be looking at it?

'Is Shadow your watch-cat?'

'Shadow is the lab cat but roams the boat. Goodbye. Time to go.'

Abruptly, Wei Wei dismissed Kit. It was as if her patience only lasted a short time and she'd just run out.

'Close the door on your way out. I like to know where Shadow is. And get rid of those kittens.'

Wei Wei was scary. Did she mean kill the kittens? Or move them? Cats are more likeable than some people. They don't answer back. But this Shadow was a digital spy.

'Out! Too busy for visitors. Don't allow any more trauma tourists in here. The last idiots wanted me to pose for their selfies in a full HAZMAT suit.'

Did she mean Kit, the cat or the kittens, or all of them to get out? Kit backed out of the lab, holding three squirming kittens. The cat had already gone.

'You take the first aid kit, I'll take the kittens,' offered Lab Rat 1, the taller of the two. 'I like baby animals. I'll look after them out of Wei Wei's sight.'

They swapped. The kittens squirmed and one clawed Kit's hand, leaving a little scratch of red.

'What's a HAZMAT suit?' Kit asked.

'A nightmare to get on and work in.'

'Should I be wearing one here?' Kit was nervous.

'Wei Wei is VERY careful. But we just wear masks and gloves at present. A biohazard suit protects against chemical and biological hazards.'

'What about kitty litter?' And then he wished he hadn't asked.

'Just another new hazard.'

Lab Rat 1 vanished down the passageway as Wei Wei called after Kit.

'Come back only if you have any ideas I can use. Can't fix problems if I have to spend time being polite to people all the time. This garbage patch project is not trash, it's scientific bio-treasure to recycle. And it needs ALL my time and attention.'

As they moved away from the lab, Frederick sort-of apologised. 'Sorry. She's worried about Cal's test results. AND she's trying to work out how to re-use plastic and stuff. Gets a bit involved. Got deadlines. Keep the first aid kit for now, you might need it for the kitten scratch.'

'What's a trauma tourist?'

'Depends who you ask. Just a bunch of rich people gawking at others' problems. Disguised as aid.'

'Why do they pay to "shadow" refugees?'

'They visit places like disaster sites where tragic things have happened. But they donate money or buy things, and the locals, like us, need that. We usually only have to put up with them for a few hours. Long enough to take their selfies to show the folks at home.'

'How do the real refugees feel about them?'

'Like animals in a zoo.'

'My mum Steffi talks about the refugees on her podcast.'

'Officially, your mum is also a refugee. She was in Camp 13. With some of the people on board here now, but –'

'I knew that. With the translator and Wei Wei. But she's a bit different from them.'

In his head, Kit drew a scavenger bird. Like that intelligent elf owl that feeds on insects. That was Wei Wei.

Should he draw Shadow the cat? He could include the tiny spy camera around the cat's neck. Was Shadow spying on Wei Wei's research? Or was Wei Wei spying on others? On the lab rats? Kit wondered who was skilled enough to set up a surveillance camera. And why.

⌐

4

Flashback: The Start-Up

Bolour's defence of her idea, recorded for the UN investigation. (Unidentified listener occasionally queries or comments.)

Having a photographic memory is useful for an interpreter. I remember conversations. And faces.

[Interpreter Bolour's voice is thoughtful and sad.]

I remember that night in the dreadful tent of Camp 13 when we began the start-up. For our Garbage Patch State. Wei Wei was fed up. Showed me her latest rejection. She'd been moved down the waitlist for a visa, again. She'd been trying to do everything the right legal way for years, and others had queue-jumped ahead of her. Illegals. With fake documents and reasons. Plus some genuine recent disaster victims. They took precedence.

What happened next?

Something worse. Wei Wei genuinely did the best for her patients. All voluntary. In Camp 13 she was respected. Reluctantly she had

45

operated on a risky patient with a major brain tumour. Unfortunately, he was one of the deposed royal family. She was forced to operate by his political connections. He died. Wei Wei was blamed for his death. She had no choice. She was the only doctor available with any surgical skills in the camp. But his political connections condemned her. Wei Wei despaired about her patient's death and her own future. She knew they needed to make an example of her.

So what happened?

She was moved to the bottom of the list. I got a 'no' too. Other refugees got rejections as well. We were desperate. I suggested, 'Let's try a different way. Maybe you could set up a kind of Climate Repairs Shop near the garbage patch? If you could invent something to patent and trade, you … we … could build our own state.'

Wei Wei was realistic. She said there were lots of failed utopias. And she didn't want to add to them. I tried to convince her that she had the science know-how. Activists here could pivot from politics to pollution. She could get a model team together.

Wei Wei suggested to me, 'Isn't "pivot" the current political jargon for changing your mind after a stuff-up?'

I agreed that I have to translate 'pivot' a lot. Chosen as Word of the Year for that dictionary. Just about every disaster aid meeting with the bureaucrats justifying local freedom fighters stealing food donations and selling them on the black market to the victims. Stuff-ups. Political expediency. Called pivoting.

Weeks before, Wei Wei had mentioned the garbage patch

existed and I'd checked who owned the garbage patch area. No-one, legally.

Wei Wei was so frustrated, she took up the idea. I hoped she might. It distracted her from political blame when the patient died and the regime blacklisted her. I didn't have her scientific background. But I was busier than most in the camp because I was called to interpret so often. Unpaid. Unrecognised. 'Just a refugee.' And it wasn't leading anywhere. So much waste in Camp 13. Boredom. Frustration. Hope fading. A recipe for revolution. And the young people like Cal just filling in time. Learning habits of nothingness. Or getting into trouble. Lost lives.

Wasted.

Not totally. But if we found a legal space, someone like Cal could be trained.

Maybe.

In the camp, Wei Wei was still the medic for refugees and for staff. She treated anyone who needed help. Even the camp security guards. Nobody cared if she was legal or not. They just needed her skills.

Meanwhile Wei Wei played with my idea.

'Look at this. Could we use a boat as a base lab? For experiments close to the garbage patch?' I asked. I skimmed through my tablet and showed Wei Wei the YouTube clip of Frederick's boat and solo living off-grid. Someone had filmed him for a series a few years ago.

Was it his partner, Max, in the background? Then there was a close-up for the double interview. Frederick looked a bit embarrassed, as if he wanted to stay in his own quiet life and was avoiding the camera at the same time as being proud of his carpentry in a tiny space. His partner definitely didn't want to be interviewed. Max turned away from the camera. Shyness or something to hide from a murky past? Was he on a wanted list somewhere? Or just that it was meant to be solo off-grid living?

'If we make the garbage patch into our own nation we could recycle from the garbage patch ... and issue visas because we're a state? Is that what you're suggesting?'

What happened next? Try to use Wei Wei's words as you remember them.

Wei Wei said, 'What about the Law of the Sea? Don't countries have control of the waters a certain distance from their coastlines?'

'Yes. Could act in our favour. Can rubbish have a coastline?'

'That should keep the lawyers busy arguing for years. They're always having Treaty meetings to change the rules, but ... Where is this Frederick's boat?'

'Just outside the garbage patch.'

'So many plastics could be recycled. But it would take time to experiment. You mean we should live there?'

'Temporarily.'

'Who'd want to?'

'I don't mean ON the garbage. Nearby.'

WASTED?

'Walk on water?'

'No, some kind of boat ... or a fleet of them.'

'How close?'

'Close enough to claim the legal space ... You wouldn't have to be anchored. You could circle. Like satellites.'

That got Wei Wei's interest. 'While we take bio-samples?'

'Why not?'

Later, most assumed it was all Wei Wei's idea. That happens to me a lot. Others take the credit. But I knew we needed something to trade or we wouldn't survive. Utopia is a myth. Power is about global economics. Trade in scarce commodities.

All those Middle Eastern and Asian medieval cities that rose and fell. All about being on trade routes. Today, intellectual property matters more than slaves, furs, gold or spices. Bio-climate repair is currency. So is water and waste. Others might argue we did this to save the planet. I knew it was for our survival. Refugees were vulnerable unless they had something to trade. After World War 2 German nuclear scientists were given an American haven for their brainpower. If there was an eco-bio trade, Wei Wei had the knowledge ...

We just had to start up. So we did. But it was my original idea.

⏜

5

Grace, Queen of Digital and the Lingo Ringo

'Are you Grace? Frederick told me to find you earlier and I went to the wrong deck. I've got to get a ring.'

'You found me. Well done ... although, the garbage dump is on some navigation maps now. Especially since they started monitoring where the rubbish was coming from and going to. And our satellite boats are a bit of an open secret since there are so many refugees.'

'Yes.'

'A shantyboat is a small crude raft, but ours isn't ... it's an add-on ...'

Was she joking? This shantyboat was SO small. And the garbage patch was in a BIG ocean. And Kit was proud that he'd found that by himself, even if Steffi's directions were super vague.

'Did you have any navigation hassles getting here?'

'Mum told me the directions, so I wasn't sure I'd find it.'

'Your mother claims she's a clairvoyant but that doesn't help much with navigation.'

As her son, he understood that.

Initials were like a code and if you knew what they meant, you were in the team. Kit knew how to use a GPS. And understood what it meant. But other initials he had to guess or ask.

Surrounded by screens in her cabin nook, Grace was sort of nerdish, even if her eyes looked naked without glasses. But she had lots of deep, dark brown wrinkles. On board most people wore sunglasses on the deck and the lab rats had protective safety glasses. Despite her mega screen time, Grace must have excellent 20/20 vision. At least she wasn't as scary as Wei Wei. Kit smoothed his well-bandaged hand. Wei Wei definitely passed First Aid 101, but ...

'No streets here. Like an onboard maze of dead ends.'

Was it rude to criticise where they were living on the shantyboat? Their home. Even if it was temporary. When did temporary become permanent? How long had they been here? And how long would he be stuck here?

'Catch this, Kit.'

It was a tight squeeze on board this craft and even worse with a bandaged hand in a cabin nook. And so far, due to clumsiness, he'd knocked over more than his share. Grace threw something tiny and round as Kit stretched, and for once caught it first time in his outstretched hand. 'Ah!' So proud of that.

'It's a ring.' Kit rolled the ring around in his hand. Translucent. Blues, green lights. Dials. 'It hums. It's like ... beautiful ... Nose ring? Toe? Ear? Wedding ring? Tummy ring?'

Fooling around out of nervousness, Kit pretended to wear it under his nose, on his ears and in his belly button. Over his clothes.

'It's not just a piece of art. Or jewellery.'

'Really?'

'This is Mark 2. A later version of the one we have patented,' Grace cautioned. 'On my shantyboat you only get one to try out. If you lose that, you're banned. I'm sure you've heard of the earlier translation device for interpreting one language to another?'

'Sure.'

'This is better. Not just for kids. Or simple phrases. Simultaneously translates every known language within a designated area. Ad free. Once it's trialled with people like you, we'll patent Mark 2 and 3. With a few optional extras.'

'People like me?'

'Everybody who is not a scientist. Or doesn't think like one.'

Kit thought Grace had too high an opinion of scientists. It was just one form of thinking. His dad couldn't even remember birthdays or to turn off the stove. Even if he did understand other important stuff. And was willing to say so in public even if it made him unpopular.

'Is this your main job?'

'I do pollucon shifts too. For visa credits.'

'You mean like from here? Onto the garbage patch?'

Kit wasn't sure what to call the *Satellite Freddie* vessel. This was more of an over-crammed apartment on water, with green creepers dangling in places where you might trip.

'Yes.' Then she added, 'And if you can understand how to work it without me giving you instructions, then there's hope for the rest of the world. I need to know if ordinary non-techies could work it within a few minutes.' Grace had a no-nonsense voice and you got the feeling that it was best not to argue with her. A bit like Wei Wei. Very focused on solving problems. People were second priority and just the means to getting issues sorted. Had they all been similar to start with, or was it living on this shantyboat that made them serious problem-solvers? Might it affect him? Change him? Probably not.

Kit had a fiddle with the ring. He had small hands, so it fitted better on his thumb than his ring finger. He was determined to show Grace that even if he was the worst tester, he could do it faster than she expected ...

He fiddled with increasing desperation. It beeped. What had he turned on? Or turned off?

'The ring is a mini device with an extension so all the

refugees can understand each other, immediately. Important, so if we have an emergency, we all know ASAP.'

'I can read in English. What if a user can't read the instructions?'

'Follow the diagrams.'

'Where?'

'I haven't drawn them yet.'

'Maybe I could help? I like drawing.' Kit didn't mention he'd already sketched Grace in his head as a manta ray. Intelligent and perceptive, with fins like wings ... Usually he drew people as animals. But out here, for some of them marine creatures seemed like ... a better fit. Like giant crab Mohammed walking sideways. He was powerful inside his shell.

'Maybe.' Dr Grace didn't sound convinced. 'See if you can work it out first and then draw the instructions.'

'What's your main job here, Grace?'

'Comms. Linking the satellite rafts. But with a security code so others don't pinch our ideas before we can patent them.'

'Much of that?'

'Yes, it's called eco-espionage.'

Kit remembered the body-cam on the cat. Was that espionage? Who was spying on Wei Wei and why? 'Many cameras on board?'

'A few, in unexpected places. If you notice them, let me know. But we also have other devices.'

'Do you want them to be noticed?'

Grace ignored that question.

'What else do you do?' Kit was sure he'd work out the ring, VERY soon. He fiddled more slowly.

'I'm a quizzaholic. My hobby. I do quizzes for fun. We play Trivial Pursuit sometimes in the galley. I used to write the answers. And then the questions.'

'Isn't that cheating?'

Nearly got the ring on! He didn't have a clue what Trivial Pursuit was.

'Depends. But you can do it the other way around.'

Unsure whether she meant the ring or the quiz, Kit got the ring in place. 'I've got it.'

'Eighty-seven seconds. I've had quicker, and slower ...'

Kit sighed with relief. 'What was the best time?'

'Wei Wei. Ten seconds. But she's MENSA material.'

What was he supposed to do with the ring now? And was MENSA an insect or a disease? He could understand Grace most of the time as they were using the same language, but ... keeping up was a challenge. Did the Great Garbo use all the extensions on the ring?

'Not yet,' Grace replied with a smile. 'The Great Garbo could easily start World War 4 every time she opens her mouth. She's outspoken and a diplomatic challenge. Or she could start Peace 101. They don't need to read her thoughts, she tells them.'

Then Grace was off on another subject. A coincidence that

Grace answered HIS unspoken thoughts? Did this ring have a superpower she wasn't telling him about? These asylum seekers were seriously bright.

Mohammed knocked at the cabin door. 'Brought you something, Grace.'

'Mohammed's been testing something for me,' Grace explained.

The muscly man looked a bit embarrassed. 'Not that, isn't sorted yet. I brought you a mug of hot soup before you do your shift. It gets cold out there.'

'Thanks.' Grace was surprised.

BANG! Suddenly there was a loud noise from the deck above them, like an explosion.

Immediately, Mohammed hit the floor. But he kept the mug of soup upright. Grace helped him up gently as the soup sloshed. He was so frightened his hands trembled.

'It's only Frederick fixing the generator. And we didn't spill much of that soup ... I can still drink it.' Grace's voice was so encouraging. 'If you're okay, I'll see you later, Mohammed.'

He left. Then Grace explained, 'Mohammed had a really bad time on the smugglers' boats. An overcrowded refugee boat in bad weather is a bad experience, anyway. He lost his family on that last voyage. An explosion. The boat blew up. He doesn't talk about it much. Now any unexpected noises worry him.'

Kit sort of understood. People were often different on the inside. Mohammed looked so strong outside.

⌐

'Heard of the floating islands of the Uros?' asked Grace.

'No. Where are they?' Kit replied. He'd mopped up the soup stains.

'Peru.'

'Were you a refugee there?'

'Sort of. More like research. I went there because Lake Titicaca is the highest altitude lake in the world.'

Why go up so high, when there was plenty of water at sea level to float on? Would it sound ignorant if he asked about a place he couldn't spell without Spellcheck, which she probably invented since she was the Queen of Digital? Was she just good at reading people's body language or did she have a digital advantage? And he didn't seem to be able to understand the way she thought. She knew what he thought. But he didn't know what she thought. Maybe she just had more experience reading people because she was old-ladyish?

'Artificial reef islands. Locals build them from reeds called totora.' Grace powered on. Like most people on board, Grace was passionate about whatever subject caught her interest. Exciting in one way. Was that the cause or effect of being here? How much would he change while living here? He'd been with Dad's speed of working and ways of thinking on the mainland for years. Dad always asked why, but did it slowly. This was different.

'Oh. You were checking out fake islands?'

'Wasn't thinking of satellite islands then. That came later. Just interested in how the locals had to keep re-thatching or they'd go under. Sometimes islands merged with others or even disappeared, so the locals had to move fast.'

'Sounds like work.'

'Means they don't waste time fighting or going to war. Have time for other discoveries or inventions. Sounds sensible to me.'

Kit thought he'd prefer fighting to housework. And thatching the sinking fake ground where you stood seemed worse than sweeping forever.

'What did they eat?'

So far no-one had mentioned food around here on *Satellite Freddie*. Except Steffi talking about getting supplies.

'Fish, and they kept ibis birds for eggs. Later they had a few cattle. But a big storm wiped them out.'

'Could that happen here?'

'Maybe. But they started again and went hi-tech. Solar panels instead of open flames. Solar to charge TV and radio. Even one island for a toilet or latrines.'

'Yuck.'

'Young people left. Oldies sell handicrafts to tourists now.'

'Were you a tourist?'

'Not exactly.'

'What were you doing?'

'Early digital nomad. Government security.'

Kit knew what that might mean. No further answers. His dad was good at blocking that kind of job question before he went maverick with his science research. And critics attacked him. Government investigation. Which government? Doing what? Rebels or freedom fighters? 'Same people; different labels,' Dad said ages ago. 'Depends whether you ask them before or after the uprising.'

'What did you find out?'

'No written history. Spoke Pukina language originally. That's why Bolour and I started talking about vanishing languages. If it's not written, it needs to be preserved in some way. And it's why instant digital translation matters now.'

'Like here?'

'A bit different and that's what gave me an idea.' Grace flicked on her Digital Lingo Ringo. Press in twice and twist. Like a child-safe screw top jar. Kit watched closely so he'd remember how to do it. Earlier, he'd fiddled so much he forgot the sequence he fluked. 'Unlike old versions, this covers all languages in use and a few lost ones. Instantaneously. Plus bonus skills.'

'Who can use it?'

'We've patented Mark 1, with royalties to the Wasted community.'

'Why not a watch or, like on your leg ...?'

'A pedometer? Been done. Jails use a leg tracker to monitor outside prisoners. Keep them under supervision.'

Dad told him once that in the olden days there were ship prison hulks. And convicts in leg irons. Luckily this shantyboat was a free sort of place, even if the sleep nooks were a bit like cells but with a few of Frederick's tiny decorations to look at in the wood.

'How did you know the words in all languages?'

'Other refugees had to help me to say them. But some just messed around and said, "It's worse than being a GPS voice. I won't do it." So I said, "If you want your language included, others need to hear your voice." "Not today, we're going fishing," they said.'

'What did you do then?' asked Kit.

'I left out the ones who went fishing. Just chose ones who volunteered. We've got a few language gaps. Mainly the stubborn, stupid ones. They're going to die out a bit faster. We were trying to give everyone a turn but then a few were lazy ... which you're not supposed to say ... In utopia it's meant to be perfect, but it isn't. That's where Wei Wei and I disagree. Dystopia is the reality.'

Kit guessed it was an opposite. Dys-topia ... Like 'dissing' was a put-down. He didn't know much about that. But he did know about food and he was getting really hungry now.

'Have you ever ... like ... used ... dystopia as a clue on your crosswords? Or quizzes?'

'Not yet.'

'Or answers that are food? Like hamburger? Or rice rolls? Or ... even green vegetables? Like spinach or broccoli? What about ice cream flavours?' Kit was always hungry, but now he felt really, really hollow. Talking about food was the next best thing. 'What about your tourists staying here. Do you feed them too?'

Grace laughed. 'Of course. Most are on the other shantyboats. They only stay a few hours or maybe one or two nights. A few climate-refugee islanders from the Low Countries stay longer and they work, not just take selfies. Haven't you found the galley yet? Our layout is a bit different from the Uros.'

'Different?' How many ways could a floating home fit as many as possible in limited space? He just had to listen, ask questions politely, and think about anything except filling his stomach.

'The Uros are about 70 rafts, made of floating islands. Some families own motorboats. Tourists paying to stay for a night even have a radio station that plays music through the day. We wanted Wasted to use the best ideas and build it even better.'

'Is our galley better?'

'Yes.'

Kit just needed to find it. His stomach was really empty. This conversation was more like a boring lesson. Time for a snack. How could he get the questions around to food?

'Why don't the floating islands sink? I know if I eat too much before swimming I might sink. I'm not going swimming for a bit, so maybe we could ...?'

Grace probably knew what he was thinking, but she kept explaining ...

'Totora reeds are tied together, layered, then anchored by driving eucalyptus stakes attached to rods into the bottom of the lake. Problem here. Our ocean is so much deeper.'

'Yeah.' Kit remembered his recent arrival. He'd been worried then that he'd end up on the bottom of the ocean. He preferred drawing fish to living with them. He didn't mind eating them either, with chips.

'How long do islands last?'

'Some fakes have just been created for military reasons in the China Sea. Not sure how long they'll last. Uros? About 30 years if well made.'

In 30 years, Kit would be REALLY old. If he was still around. And found something to eat SOON! He couldn't imagine an old version of him. Would he be the same person under his wrinkly skin? Would he be wrinkly? And really really really skinny.

If he stayed out on this shantyboat for decades, he would. Luckily, Grace was super keen on floating islands, not sinking ones.

'Turn my pin-up wall around.' Grace pointed to the cabin wall behind her computer screen.

Kit fiddled with the wall, swung it out and then managed to flip it. On the other side was a giant, old-style world map. With pins stuck in it. Like a flat map pin cushion.

'All fake islands. Man-made. And I've pinned all I've visited.'

'What are the crosses?'

'Guess.'

'Food supply chains?'

'Ones that sank.'

'Oh. Did the people have passports? On the islands that sank?'

'No. You have to be a state before you can issue a passport. Or a visa. That's why Wasted will be different.'

'Unsinkable?

'I didn't say that. Although Frederick is a careful builder. And he's trained a few of the newcomers.'

'Did you ever have a passport from somewhere else?'

Since his mum had lost her passport, he'd googled visas. There seemed to be lots of different kinds. Was a humanitarian visa a kind one? He wasn't sure what a bridging visa linked.

'Look at this.' Grace opened a drawer and showed him an old-style, cardboardy passport with embossed gold letters. Kit had never seen so many official exit and entry stamps in so many languages. The ink was murky and hard to read on some. Upside down and sideways. Stuck with stamped, used visas.

'Epic.'

'Filled my passport with entry and exit travel stamps and extra pages. I went everywhere. And now I need a Wasted passport and visa to travel again!'

Why did Grace need a Wasted passport and visa? Why couldn't she renew the old one? Maybe she wanted a new ID? Did she look different now? Lots of refugee camps had people wanting a new ID – Steffi told him that.

'How come you need a new one?'

'Work it out for yourself.'

Maybe he'd think better after a meal? Had she been a spy? Or undercover? Could he ask her that?

'Are you there, Kit? Your mum was looking for you.' Frederick's voice came closer.

'Coming. Thanks, Grace, for the ring ... and everything.' Kit pushed the ring on firmly. No way did he want to lose it.

As they walked down the corridor, Frederick explained, 'Grace's experimental rings didn't work at first. Users lost them in the garbage patch, or down the latrine. So Grace made them waterproof. And added security.'

'Can your ring read my mind?' Kit sort-of joked.

'Maybe. There would need to be some worthwhile thoughts for it to find.' Frederick laughed. 'And I'd need to press the right sequence. Let's eat.'

'You CAN read my mind.'

Could he smell pizza? Kit's head was full of takeaway signs

for food. Rich. Colourful. Tasty. Spicy. Hot. He could almost smell and taste the food. Cheesy. Toasty. Smelly in just the right way.

⤳

6

Galley

'Food okay?'

Something savoury was cooking on the stove in a frypan. Frederick checked and turned the heat off. The almost burning smell of onions filled the galley.

Meanwhile, they were having spiced split pea soup and multiple 'tuna roll' snacks in the galley. Plus help-yourself strawberries from the pot plants. Beans, herbs and healthy green stuff like spinach, broccoli, peppers and weird lettuce for salads. Frederick definitely knew his way around the solar-powered fridge and the built-in stove. Storage baskets on shelves too, so you could quickly find what was inside, like rice or oatmeal or spices. Kit was relieved at seeing the well-provisioned stores in neat drawers and cupboards when Frederick opened them. Everything was labelled and sealed in jars or containers. No plastic! Enough for months. He needn't have worried about going hungry if he couldn't catch fish.

'This is smoko,' announced Frederick. 'Want another helping?'

Kit shook his head. At last he was full. His stomach felt so firm. And he could last for another few hours without more food.

'Do you smoke?'

'No.'

'So, why's it called smoko?'

Frederick said, 'Not breakfast, not lunch, sort of in between. Leftover custom from building tradies starting really early in freezing weather, then taking a break for a smoke mid-morning and a hot meal. Do that on the Antarctic bases too. It's the one meal everybody has together so the boss has a chance to share any news or tell us what to do.'

'So where is everybody?'

'They've already had smoko. We take turns cooking. What can you make?'

'Depends what's in the fridge.'

'Then have a look.'

Just as Kit opened the fridge, Theo burst into the cabin.

'Sorry, left the eggs and onions on again.'

How could Theo not smell the onions burning?

'Hi Kit. You know I'm Theo. Didn't have time to chat properly earlier.'

As a well-muscled giant, he filled all the narrow space, but he moved lightly on his feet. Deft movements. That fall from the mast must have been embarrassing for him. Kit was used to falls. Normal. As the open door took up too much space, and beeped, Kit closed the fridge, which was covered in smiley-face magnets and family photos.

'Did they all work here?'

'Just a sample. Wasted's history is growing. Most went on to other places once they got visas.'

Theo interjected, 'Never imagined I'd be a pin-up for reality TV. Would you like to see my poster? It's pinned on the galley wall. Damn. Someone has covered it again. Let's turn this around.'

Deftly Theo flipped the versatile wall. Instead of photos of 'Weirdest Thing I Found in the Ocean', duty lists, maps and 'How many days to go before ...', there was a floor to ceiling photo of Theo's Olympic appearance, with dates, times and the refugee flag.

'Meet the real me. Want my autograph?'

'Why would Kit want that?'

'Sell it on eBay? Sports memorabilia?'

'I used to have your poster on my bedroom wall. After your Olympic victory,' Kit admitted.

Theo's smile grew. 'Who else was on your wall?'

'Cartoons of animals and marine creatures. Like salties – saltwater crocodiles.'

'Oh,' Theo seemed disappointed.

'I could draw you now,' offered Kit, unsure what to say about the overwhelming 'Theo' photo in such a tiny space, as well as the breathing, moving Theo. The poster was bigger than the man. Double Theo. That was a bit much.

'Draw from life?'

'Yeah, sort of caricature. Or a cartoon. Frederick is a smoked mackerel.'

'That's a compliment, I think.' Frederick smiled. 'What about the others on board?'

'Haven't drawn them all yet. And I don't always show them to the subjects.'

'Wei Wei?'

'Scavenger bird. Super intelligent elf owl feeds on insects. Had to google that.'

Theo laughed. 'You got that right. She's a cluey lady. Maybe you could draw me and I'll give it to my girlfriend if I ever get another one. Always have trouble deciding on gifts.'

'Why?'

'I never buy my girlfriends perfume or flowers. I can't smell the scent,' admitted Theo.

'But the girlfriends can,' suggested Kit.

'I mean I can't smell the samples to choose the best ones,' added Theo. 'That's why I'm no good at cooking either. We'll have to get some chooks on board, Frederick. I've burnt so many eggs. And frypans.'

'That's true.' Kit scraped the burnt pan, then soaked it. Some of the onions had stuck to the bottom.

'Don't you cook by taste?' asked Kit, intrigued. He LOVED

food. And he cooked for Dad too. But lately Dad had lost his taste for food and didn't eat much.

Theo admitted, 'I mean I burn things because I forget they're still cooking. And I don't smell the burnt pan until too late.'

'Yeah.' Those eggs were very frazzled. And the onions had lost it.

'Beyond recycling? The pan, I mean. Not the eggs – they're cactus.'

Frederick disagreed about the extinct pan. 'I'll clean that up, and plant some herbs in it,' he offered. 'I did that with the other one Theo burnt. Not sure about chooks on board. Space limited. If you've finished eating, Kit, let's watch the news, in the cabin next door.' Frederick checked the stove burner. 'Not working properly. Have to find a part to replace this soon. I'm sure there are back-ups in the lockers.'

After clearing up their meal plates, they moved next door.

Theo peered at the screen.

'Our "Clean Oceans" campaign is going well. But we need a better address for where we live.'

Kit agreed. '"Wasted" is weird. "Great Garbage Patch, The Ocean", doesn't work either.'

'"Wasted" sounds a bit insulting. Or drunk. Utopia is a perfect place. This isn't, but we're working with what we've got. Wei Wei is so keen on creating a perfect society. Trouble is, none of us is perfect. If you call a place "Utopia", "Paradise" or "Heaven", visitors are always disappointed,' Theo said.

'How about "Boring"? Then they'd always be impressed it was better than they expected. Might have a town to twin with on the other side of the world. What is the most boring place you know?' Kit asked.

'Here.'

Theo laughed as Frederick said, 'That chopper delivery was for Messi. Do you know where he is?'

Theo shook his head.

'Take those other boxes on deck down to Wei Wei's lab if you're going that way, Theo? She was waiting on some results from the mainland. Ever since the tourists gave us the gift of Covid and Cal got sick, Wei Wei has been double-testing everything. She gave Cal anti-virals, but then Cal fell and broke her arm, which got infected. So she needed antibiotics as well. Just one thing after another.'

Curious, Kit lifted the seat and saw the space underneath was crammed with tightly packed supplies and a few engine parts, all labelled. Frederick believed in being prepared for breakdowns mid-ocean. Maybe they could be self-sufficient for months on *Satellite Freddie*. But could they all get along with each other in such small spaces?

He missed Dad. They were used to living together on the mainland. It was ordinary and easy. He wanted that back.

Living with strangers was different. You had to fit in with them all the time.

⌐

'Give me a hand, Kit.' Frederick started pulling out wrapped objects and repacking the lockers under the seats. 'I've got spare parts for the stove in here somewhere. Just got time to fix it quickly now.'

'Do you carry back-ups for everything?' Kit tried to read the labels in the hard-to-read writing. Was SCOVE, stove? Curly writing? Maybe a bad speller?

'Yes. Usually two spares. Is there more than one kid in your family? Any spares? Got any brothers or sisters?'

'Nah. Mum says she didn't really want me, but now I'm here, she's okay with that.'

'Are you?'

Kit shrugged. 'Lived with my dad until a month ago. He had to go into hospital then. He brought me up. Made a great spag bol. Except when he added healthy spinach. And tried to hide it.'

'So he won't be joining us?'

Time to change the subject.

'Why have you got that "Frederick" tatt on your arm? In case you forget who you are?'

'Mmm. Can't remember. Got my date of birth in Roman numerals on my bum.'

'Why?'

'Just in case.'

'In case of what?'

'I'll leave that to your imagination.' Another adult phrase which meant Frederick didn't know. But if he used Roman numerals that was sort of Latin ...

⤚

On the top deck, wafting a blue veil, Steffi was tip-toe dancing. Surprisingly she was a really graceful dancer. She had to tip-toe because there were so many obstacles like ropes and boxes and changeover equipment for the refugee crew.

Theo clapped to the rhythm. Kit stood beside the lone, bewildered trauma tourist who was pressed up against the railing, taking up as little space as possible, as Steffi leapt and gyrated around him.

The trauma tourist tried to explain to Kit that he'd just returned from the garbage patch circuit, seen the lab rats testing, inspected recycled sleeping bags and satellite boat gardens, and was 'shadowing' Steffi and participating in her podcast for the next hour until his transport returned. He'd donated to see a day in the life of Wasted community refugees ... at a relevant site.

'Is that veil meant to be waves?' asked the bewildered trauma tourist.

Kit couldn't think of an answer that didn't make his mother look ridiculous.

So he made up one.

'Symbolic of refugees crossing the oceans.'

'Of course,' nodded the tourist. 'To get away from trauma. Steffi mentioned that in the podcast. She spoke so effectively about the importance of refugees needing permanent homes and visas. Some have had such extreme experiences. At least I can donate money to help. I'll be leaving soon.'

Kit didn't know what to say.

The tourist seemed to be genuine about wanting to help, but ... Maybe second-hand tragedies were easier. You could opt out when it suited. Not everyday living.

Steffi did another twirl and bowed in front of the tourist with a flourish of her veil.

'Thank you for coming. Your transport will be here soon.'

Steffi's dancing didn't seem to have much to do with recycling biowaste. Or learning ways of stopping refugees from being seen like victims.

If it was just Kit and Mum, they mostly got along, but when other people were around, her 'marine therapy' was just so embarrassing. He always had to think of excuses.

'Mum, do you have to do it here, now?' Kit whispered. 'We're supposed to be working shifts.'

'I WAS working, escorting the trauma tourist. He paid well and that helps the others. I know your dad would say that my dancing doesn't help the dolphins or the other marine life ... but it makes me feel better. Want to dance with me, Kit?'

'No way.'

The trauma tourist backed off, just in case.

'Rangi would, but he's away ... back on the mainland.'

'Maybe that's why,' Kit muttered. He'd wondered for a while if Rangi really existed or if Mum had made him up as a spirit boyfriend so she could claim his 100% support whenever she did something others objected to.

Hard to argue with an invisible, mythical superhero.

'Where were you earlier, Mum? Did you go to see Dad?'

'No. I was sorting the supplies for the other shantyboats.' Steffi's face looked sad. 'He's been a good man, your dad. A bit of a maverick scientist, but he realised things others didn't. Found solutions. Not his fault we split up.'

Kit wished he'd stayed with his father. He really wanted to. But Dad had ordered him to leave. Dad promised to call if and when he wanted Kit to come. Kit worried that Dad would be too ill to do anything by then.

'He's being well looked after.' Mum changed the subject. 'Did you find the sleep nook? I embroidered your name. And I'm sure you'll find useful work here and things you can draw. It's just for a while, until I earn the visa for us. And Grace has a Lingo Ringo for you.'

'Thanks, Mum. I've got it already.' Kit held up his thumb. Better fit than his ring finger, but still a bit loose.

Kit usually spoke as though his mother was an amusing friend. Only way he could handle her.

'Time to go?' he asked.

Kit remembered what Dad said when he left for the shantyboat, 'Always meant well, but ... "famously indecisive"; that's Steffi. But she does love you and our family.'

Mum had trouble making up her mind. She flitted from one thing to the next. Dad wasn't sure how long she'd last on the satellite rafts, so he wanted Kit to stay. Since Steffi was really good at making 'craft' type things, recycling trash could be her climate repair thing. Or not.

'Pollucon next?' Kit asked.

〜

7

Dragon Boat Mishap

The sun vanished. Dark clouds appeared. Luckily the trauma tourist's lift home to the mainland had already been organised by Steffi and he'd gone in one of the shared boats. Just in time.

'Storm warning!' someone shouted.

Suddenly *Satellite Freddie* was moving more than usual. Up and down. Sideways. Up again. Kit braced his legs. To balance, he grabbed the pot plant shelf rather than the creepers. Luckily it looked Frederick-built and sturdy. He held on.

Boom. Boom! BOOM! 'That's not thunder. What is it?'

'Trouble. You'll find out very soon. Here comes Messi,' said Steffi.

First the drumming was heard. And then the chanting. Kit couldn't make out the words at first. Just a chain of sounds magnified across the waves. There was a primitive beat that went through your head. Energy was approaching.

'Who are they?'

'You'll find out now.'

A curious crowd grew on the *Satellite Freddie* deck from

those already on board. Even Dr Wei Wei and her lab rats joined them from below.

'Wow! It's a dragon boat!'

Across the water, the throbbing sound magnified above the discarded flotsam and jetsam of the garbage patch.

This place was a real transport hub. Kayaks, canoes, choppers, rafts and now ... a dragon boat! Weird to see a vessel emerge from the haze around the garbage patch, as if the dragon boat were coming from an earlier century or another world.

'That's Messi?' asked Kit. 'Is he a refugee too?'

'Depends who's asking. Messi is a religious con artist,' Frederick muttered. 'But he won't tell you that. He's very persuasive and people believe him. Wants to be Head of State so he can skim off any money.'

'Opportunistic,' added Wei Wei. 'Like helping Lex with the contract for mining the ocean bed minerals for the Prime Minister from the Pacific Islands. Getting the ocean licence.'

'Minerals?' Theo looked up sharply. 'What minerals?'

'Forget it. Shouldn't have mentioned that. No proof yet.' Wei Wei looked embarrassed, as if she'd been caught giving away secrets.

'Does Messi usually work here or is this his first visit?'

'Messi is a regular, but not always a worker. To change the subject ... human powered watercraft,' Theo muttered. 'Magnificent muscles.'

'Dragon boat,' Wei Wei explained. 'I rowed in one when I was a girl. Fun, but hard work. Usually have more rowers. This must be the cut-price version.'

'Here comes the God ... of Small Things,' commented the taller lab rat.

Two little watercraft with drums escorted the dragon boat in a ragged formation with banners dipping between them. Standing on the bow of the dragon boat was a silhouette with a megaphone and the light behind him. His tree trunk legs braced against the movement of the craft in stocky outline. But as he came closer, and the light dimmed behind, Kit could see the hairy, towering man with contained energy behind his eyes, who looked like an action movie reject and likely to lose balance any minute. Up and down.

'Messi is a bit short on supporters and he's not even rowing himself. Typical.'

'He's telling them where to go.'

'What's different?'

'I bet that dragon boat didn't come from China's Pearl River area. That's where they originated.'

'Probably just hired. Wants to impress someone.'

Kit turned around to check. Who needed impressing? Who WASN'T impressed at this spectacle? Sounds as if the locals liked entertainment, but not Messi himself.

Behind, on the lower decks, everybody was watching the dragon boat. A few people looked impressed by the muscle power. Or were trying to read the words on the banner. But not Frederick. He was wary, checking the sky.

'Storm coming quickly.'

'Pity Messi didn't check the forecast first,' was a mutter behind Kit. 'Hope the tourist gets back safely too.'

On board, everyone checked the weather warnings more often than the time zones on various devices. Messi obviously didn't.

'Usually the dragon boats celebrated the Water God,' explained Wei Wei.

'Messi thinks he's God,' muttered Theo. 'On loan to us.'

'If you haven't been water-born, baptised ... christened ... confirmed ... and accepted the word of God, you are condemned to Hell eternally,' Messi bellowed into the microphone.

The chanting continued. Messi indicated for the drumming chorus to stop once he was centre stage in the opaque water.

Kit spelled out the letters on the banner, 'D–I–A–T–O–M ... D–E–A–T–H,' and that's what they were saying. Were they for or against? It didn't seem to matter. Just that they were loud and rhythmic and it was enticing.

Unfortunately, Messi had chosen his political moment badly, weather-wise. The waves were getting choppier. The dragon boat rowers were skilled but had trouble with Messi's erratic movements. 'I want to warn you!' He threw out his arms a lot for emphasis and the boat tipped each time.

'Look out!'

It was one of those moments when you knew what was likely to happen. The dragon boat tilted again, then capsized sideways in slow motion. Messi fell in the water, bottom first, legs and arms up. His hairy head was the last to go under water, with the dark curls vanishing.

Splash! Water spray, hard as hailstones with the minute plastic refuse, reached even the bystanders on deck who stepped back.

Most of the dragon boat rowers fell sleekly into the murky water and quickly surfaced, gulping and spluttering. The two smaller boats rocked out of control, and then righted themselves with help from the rowers.

Messi spat and choked explosively, going up and then under several times, arms flailing. Panicking, the big man noisily displaced a lot of water. 'Help me!'

Their ears deafened by water, rowers hauled themselves to the side, not realising Messi was going under again.

'Unbelievable. He can't swim,' a lab rat realised. 'Haul him out.'

Messi was subsiding into the murky water. 'Help,' he gurgled.

'We're coming, Messi.' Kit tried to remember his lifesaving classes. His brain went into super-fast mode. What could he throw to keep Messi floating? Messi was the type of frightened non-swimmer to drag his rescuer down. A lifebuoy or a life jacket? A kickboard? A rope? Hadn't seen an Esky cooler lid on deck. That might have worked.

Could Messi be reached with a stick? An oar? The towel wasn't long enough. Should Kit row the *Sardine* out to help Messi?

Others were still flailing in the water. Better to throw in some lifebuoys rather than dive. Have to keep a safe distance because Messi was panicking enough to pull him under. And he was a big man, with extra strength because he was frightened. Maybe tow him back? But a youth wasn't strong enough against a frantic man this size. If Messi grabbed him around the neck, Kit would be in real danger. Even a strong swimmer like Kit could be throttled by Messi. Luckily, Theo was likely to help and already stripping off his shoes and jacket. And he was super strong. Together, could they both deal with a panicky person wanting to grab hold? Even if it's Messi?

Kit was amazed at how fast his brain was processing options. Emergencies did that for him. It was like a flickering film of possible scenarios. Anything he did would improve Messi's chances, so he had to act. Risky, but ... no choice. Vital not to waste time. A decision was better than doing nothing. Even if he was blamed later.

'Theo!' Kit grabbed a lifebuoy from the deck and threw it in the water. Then he added a second one. Just in case. 'Theo! Shall we try together?'

Already stripping, Theo nodded. 'Tempting to leave him there, but … I'll go first.'

Instantly, Theo did a neat dive from the satellite platform, closely followed by Kit. Other rowers were struggling out of the water, unaware of Messi because they didn't have an overview from higher up on the boat deck where the lab rats gathered, encouraging them.

The lifebuoy was designed to be thrown to a person in water, to provide buoyancy. But it was bobbing around, not close enough to Messi, who was flailing around creating his own waves, which pushed it further away.

'Grab the lifebuoy, Messi.' Theo's distinctive voice carried across the water but was ignored by the drowning man.

'Over there, Messi. Grab it!'

The non-swimmer was still floundering and lashed out at them. He hit Kit in the face, but Theo turned him around, and with his greater arm strength started to tow Messi to the side of *Satellite Freddie.*

Together they grabbed Messi with practised lifesaving holds and towed him to safety.

Kit swam on the other side, helping to direct them towards the boat where a rope ladder dangled. It was hard work against the waves and a man like Messi, who wasn't helping.

'Thought you were the King of Clumsy,' panted Theo as he manoeuvred the difficult body.

'Not in the water. Steffi made sure I could swim as a toddler.'

Strong arms hauled them aboard. The stocky man, who looked as though he'd practised manhandling sheep or goats around a mountain village, grabbed Theo. It was Mohammed.

'Thanks, mate.' Theo gasped. 'Might qualify for a medal out of this, Mohammed.'

The stocky man just nodded and kept pulling.

Ignoring the rope ladder, other refugees leaned down to help and they unceremoniously hauled the big, floppy Messi over the side, where he lay on the deck gasping like a giant fish.

Leaning over the side of the upper boat deck was Steffi, looking proud.

'That's MY son,' gushed Steffi, scrambling down the steps. She wrapped her arms around Kit in a giant, wet hug. 'Your face is bruised.'

'Let me go, Mum.' Kit sort-of loved his mum, but sometimes she was SO embarrassing.

Messi still needed help. Water was dripping from him on the deck. Mohammed wrapped him in towels and blankets and then went below deck for more.

'Mum, did you know Mohammed before?' Kit asked, hoping to move his mother's attention from him and making an embarrassing fuss, again.

'Mohammed. Yes. Refugee Legal Aid didn't know what to do with him. He lost his family when the smugglers' boat was fired on. There was an explosion. Later he got a humanitarian refugee visa to the mainland, on compassionate grounds. Lost his temper one night, went to prison and his visa was revoked,' Steffi explained quietly as Kit shivered in his wet clothes.

'So what's he doing here?' His teeth were sort of moving on their own, Kit was so cold.

'He can't be sent back to his original country, it isn't there any more. Borders changed. Stateless. He was in detention for years. Not sure how he got out. He's a hard worker and always helpful. But he's hoping to get a passport from here.'

'Like you?'

'So glad I made my son Kit do his swimming lessons. Now he's a hero.' Steffi spoke loudly now for the audience on board.

The next surprise for Kit was when the Great Garbo appeared and handed him a towel. She was wearing a hoodie with her plaits sticking out and a few ribbons on them.

'Here, have my hoodie, Kit.' She took it off to reveal a thick, striped, hand-knitted jumper. 'Take your wet clothes off.'

How did she know his name?

'Thanks, but ...' Kit felt too embarrassed to strip, so he draped the hoodie around his shoulders. It smelled of peppermints.

'You're a lifesaver, Kit. That's astonishing.'

'Yeah. Got my certificates.' Kit shivered. That water was not the cleanest swim he ever had. He'd probably get the plague or something.

'That was a MIRACLE! I was saved for a higher purpose,' announced Messi in between splutters. 'Where's the Chief

Seeker? Wei Wei, did you see that miracle? Saved by divine intervention ...'

Experienced in emergencies, Dr Wei Wei had collected towels and supplies from below. Plus blankets and snooze-bags to put around the rescued people. She was dismissive of Messi's comment about a miracle.

'Today it was two lifesavers, Theo and Kit. That's skill.'

'Or a miracle?' insisted Messi.

'We're working on scientific solutions here. Proof, not superstitious mumbo jumbo.'

Messi turned back to the shivering Kit, who had decided to put on the Great Garbo's hoodie and was twisting his wet t-shirt off underneath it. 'Have you been water-born, Kit?' Baptised? Christened? Confirmed? And accepted the word of God as your Saviour?'

This big Messi was so damply hairy, his arm hair curled double, and he was so tall as he rose on his muscular legs. Amazing they'd got such a big man out of the water while he was panicking. Kit didn't have a clue what 'water-born' meant but knew this man was powerful. Or thought he was. Like a sort of religious Messiah. Hypnotic. Messi's eyes focused completely on the person he was talking to, and this time, unfortunately, it was Kit.

Messi repeated, 'Have you been water-born, Kit? Baptised?'

'Nah. Fallen in the pool a few times though.'

'So why are you here, Kit?'

'Mum ordered me to come.' Kit shivered.

'Forget about that.' Frederick was practical. 'We need to look after the survivors NOW. More towels. Hot drinks. Change of clothes.'

The Great Garbo started to rub Kit's skinny legs with another dry towel. He stepped away. 'I can do that. Thanks.' But he was still shivering uncontrollably. He knew he should go below and get dry and changed, but it was as if he was frozen inside and couldn't initiate anything. He just waited, letting them talk around him. If he went below now, what would he miss?

Meanwhile, 'thank you' didn't seem to be in Messi's vocabulary. But he did tell the rowers to make sure the dragon boat was returned on time to the rental place on the mainland or he'd be charged an extra week. And to tell them they got the date wrong, so he wanted a refund.

'That was a wasted effort, Messi. No news crews. No-one was filming for the history channel,' said Lab Rat 1 with a mischievous smile. All were relieved, and joking helped change the mood from near tragedy to normality.

'And there's not much space on our shantyboat for people who used to be dragon boat rowers. We'll have to share them around the other satellite boats.'

'They're rowing home. That's a better idea.'

Messi retorted, 'Typical! How are you going to

accommodate millions of refugees if you can't fit in extra people just for a few hours?'

Messi had the biggest of Steffi's snooze-bags around his shoulders now. He didn't seem worried about the fate of his dragon boat rowers, or his two rescuers. And a big mug of chocolate had arrived courtesy of Frederick.

'Is Messi short for Messiah? How do you know religious stuff?' Kit wasn't exactly sure what a Messiah did. Dad was agnostic and Steffi swapped religions every few months, so Kit had missed out on religious instruction as a little kid. But if he asked questions, people would look at Messi. Not at him shivering.

The smiley lab rat supported Kit, whose teeth were still chattering, in provoking Messi. 'How do you know what God thinks? Do you text God? Do you have, like … any qualifications to be a Messiah? Got any proof?'

Messi changed the subject. He was good at that. 'Give me a hand, boy. And another towel. This one is wet. And I'll have another hot chocolate, girlie.'

In her scarf and 'little girl' skirts with knitted socks and sandals home-made from recycled stuff, which looked like Steffi's craft work, the Great Garbo was an advertisement for recycling.

'It's in the galley,' said the Great Garbo. 'There's a help-yourself bar. Why don't you?'

Messi looked annoyed, as if a subject had defied royalty.

'Last time we met, you said I was inspirational, Messi.' The Great Garbo pulled down the well-worn, stretchy sleeves on her stripey jumper. As if pulling on her armour.

'I don't remember.'

'Is that why you didn't check the weather forecast? Everybody on board is always checking.'

'Now you've been water-born, Kit,' Messi declared.

'No, Kit just rescued YOU!' The Great Garbo looked straight at Messi. 'Don't take God-credit for things you didn't do.'

Kit was shocked at the Great Garbo's response. Even when Steffi was really embarrassing, he would never talk to her like that. Was the Great Garbo saying the unexpected just to stand out? Like a toddler tantrum? Or did she really want to demolish Messi?

It was surreal on deck. People had just appeared from nowhere, and were listening. Hot drinks arrived. Extra warm jackets. Their chatter was a weird kind of after party.

Shaped like a triangle, with a peaked, small head and broad hips, a woman who had been watching them closely commented, 'What is it with you, GG? Ignorance or apathy?'

'Bolour, I don't know and I don't care,' the Great Garbo replied and Kit smiled, unsure whether she was cleverly positioning those words or if it was a fluke.

She grinned.

Bolour changed techniques.

'You won't be Head of State for long. Especially if you "piss off" people. They need hope that things will improve. And you need to be diplomatic.'

The Great Garbo shrugged. 'Do you want the job, Bolour? I don't. I'm tired of it.'

'Be honest. You enjoy the attention. Constantly being asked your opinion. Featured on the front pages of international magazines and even a doco. And when you're being difficult, the media will chase you for a while, but then they get fed up. Not everything is about you. Why not compliment Theo and Kit on saving Messi?'

The Great Garbo nodded. 'Glad we've got some lifesavers on board.'

Meanwhile, the rowers had manoeuvred their boat up the right way. Only the banner had vanished into the murky depth.

'Messi is a legend in his own puddle,' the lab rats muttered.

'We didn't have the full number of rowers,' commented Messi. 'Not my fault we tipped over.'

'Never *is* Messi's fault when things go wrong. Always an evil plot,' commented Wei Wei. 'Useful to blame others when you're a poor organiser. Deflects the criticism.'

Messi overheard and shot Wei Wei a withering look.

'Your turn will come, Wei Wei.'

She ignored him. 'Gun talk from a water pistol.'

'Did you make that up? Sounds clever.' The Great Garbo smiled.

'No, it was Dr Google.'

Kit wasn't sure exactly what Wei Wei meant but knew it was an insult. Still sounded funny with so much water shaken on the deck from the dripping dragon boat rowers.

And like a show-off kid who wants the limelight back, the Great Garbo interjected, 'Can you email God, Messi? Or does it return to sender?'

'Keep that God man out of our lab,' said the shorter lab rat, with the bald head. 'He's the Dictator of Bugger All.' He winked at the shivering Kit. 'And his password of GOD is unacceptable. Too few letters. And no numbers. We were the ones who let down the rope ladder for you. Not God.'

Packing up, Wei Wei warned, 'Messi hasn't been touched by God, he's just delusional. We need scientific proof in our line of work.'

'Science may not be enough.' Stepping forward, Steffi nodded. 'I'm an intuitive. I understand many things others do not, but sometimes I forget boring domestic stuff.'

'Am I just boring domestic stuff?' Kit's teeth were still chattering despite the hot drink. He knew he should have stayed on the mainland.

'Of course you're not boring. You're my son.'

Steffi was always keen on new young people. But not one in her own family. Sometimes Kit wished she noticed him more.

'Recycle artist-refugee is an important role. My strengths are to make something artistic out of discards. And to lift spirits.'

'Entertainment over,' Wei Wei said, and headed back to her lab.

Messi was ready to keep arguing. He pointed to the 'Satellite Freddie' sign.

'That shell name for the boathouse? Can't see how it contributes much to the world economy. Anything else?'

'The snooze-bag you're wearing now.' Steffi's tone changed when defensive, and she sounded like she was pitching for a job. 'Woven backpacks. Portable tents for the homeless. I'm more of a maker. Although my ex-husband was a bit of a maverick scientist, and that's why I knew about this project. I'm the "culture" bit of eco-culture. That's important.'

'More important than what?' Kit wondered.

Messi wasn't convinced either. 'And what did Wei Wei think of that?'

'She demands proof and evidence. We don't see things the same way.'

'But you both came from Refugee Camp 13.'

'Just got caught in the wrong place at the wrong time. The borders closed and I had no visa and no passport. It was the only way I could quickly organise a home for my son, Kit, on the shantyboat. It was an emergency. Usually he lives with his dad, but that's not possible any more. And, of course, my podcast makes me an eco-influencer.'

'And how do you measure that influence?' Theo was drying

94

himself vigorously between shivers. 'The TV companies use verified ratings for viewers. *Survival* was No. 1.'

Steffi shrugged. 'Not sure. Podcasts are different. But it's my way of improving things. I don't believe in violence. I'm a pacifist.'

'So you're like the Great Garbo? Only an older version,' Messi showered droplets as he towelled his hair dry.

Steffi moved away from him in disgust but asserted, 'If I come up with recycled products that could be traded for the community, I could help get others a Wasted passport. And a visa. That's important.'

'What's a diatom?' Kit asked Messi.

'The reason we're protesting.'

〜

Much later that day, when he had some spare time, Kit would google it.

Diatoms are algae that grow in nutrient-rich waters.

Plastic quickly decomposes (it starts within a year) due to the effects of the sun and water, and ends up becoming a bad pollutant for the marine ecosystem. Toxic substances it releases are introduced into the food chain.

Soil carbon farming or 'sequestration' sucks carbon dioxide from the atmosphere and locks it in the ground, offsetting greenhouse gas emissions and at the same time improving soil. In the surrounding water, diatoms (algae that photosynthesise) grow rapidly in the nutrient-rich waters from the sea currents and those produced by the original colonising bacterium. Fish colonise the area and grow rapidly, fed by the diatoms. These fish support higher levels of carnivorous fish and mammal species, including seals.

Grounded and abandoned ships and boats drawn by the same currents and wind give access to refined resources such as copper, glass, motors (power), generators, solar panels, water tanks, etc.

It is a relatively simple process to reverse engineer plastics to produce fuels such as diesel.

Sounded really complicated. Easier if he drew the chain of events. So he did. Fish were easy to draw, but hard to get the sizes right with the algae and the diatoms. So he added a few seals. And drew arrows for the currents and greenhouse gas emissions. Then he understood it a little bit better. He preferred visuals. But still wasn't sure why Messi was against diatoms. The plastic waste was already messing up the bio-balance. Or was Messi against Wei Wei adding ingredients to the ocean to improve things?

~

8

The Great Garbo

Eventually, with the excitement of Messi's rescue over, the deck emptied as the crew went below. In the distance were other shantyboats, like shadowy blobs on the horizon. Hard to tell where the ocean ended and the sky began – the colour was the same murky grey-blue. The wind died down, and soon only Kit and the Great Garbo remained on deck.

Kit, wrapped in a thick blanket and slightly warmer now, knew he had to ask.

'How come you ended up here, GG?' He didn't want to call her the Great Garbo.

'They needed me. I'm Youth and the Future.'

Was she just recycling phrases media interviewers said? Sounded like the Great Garbo had gulped all the high-sounding phrases without even chewing. Then she threw up, vomiting them back at him.

'Youth? I'm the youngest on board,' said Kit. 'Like ... I'm younger than you ...'

'But you're not the Head of Government. I'm the Great Garbo.'

Being the youngest ones on board was all they shared, but if they were both going to live here for a while, Kit would need to find something they could talk about. He couldn't avoid bumping into her on the various decks. *Satellite Freddie* was too small to get away from anyone who annoyed you. Must have been even worse in the refugee camps. Staying there for so long ... like years. Maybe with people in the next tent who fought on the other side during wartime. Former enemies. Serious differences. Meanwhile GG was his problem. His live-in shantyboat problem. And he'd have to find a way of getting along with her.

'The Great Garbo is legally the only person to sign official documents on behalf of the State of Wasted.'

'Unreal,' Kit said. 'Too much paperwork.'

She talked of herself officially, as if the Great Garbo was another person, outside her body. Weird? Or just a way of getting things done? Giving yourself instructions. On 'how to ...' Kit wasn't sure. Living with Steffi as a mum, even part-time, meant he was used to people being a bit different and him having to fit in. Maybe the GG was just lonely, but pretended she wasn't. And was rude to keep people away or from criticising her up close.

'Are you old enough to do that? Don't you have to be 18 or 21 to be adult?' Kit challenged her.

'Have you got L plates?'

'Learner plates?'

The Great Garbo was surprised he answered her back. 'In some states you can drive at 16.'

'But you don't drive on the shantyboat. You steer a boat. And there's no space around here to drive a car.'

The Great Garbo was difficult to convince. 'Unless it's a water taxi,' she said.

Unexpectedly, they both grinned.

Watching those birds whose name he didn't know swoop over the garbage patch, Kit asked quietly, 'Are you a real refugee?'

'I ran away from my family.'

'That doesn't make you an asylum seeker. Or a refugee. What's your real name?'

'I don't use that any more.' GG looked a bit awkward.

'Why not?'

'I traded it in. At 13. I think everybody should be able to choose their own name. Especially if they don't like the one they were given.'

'So what was your old name?'

The Great Garbo paused and then said hurriedly, 'Brunhilda.'

'You're right.' Kit smiled. Then GG did too.

'Is there anything else you do like? Or want to do?'

The Great Garbo just looked at him blankly.

'What's the question you least want me to ask and what is your answer?'

GG shrugged. 'Dunno.'

What a going-nowhere, useless conversation. Even Dad's killer question didn't work. He'd never met a person like GG before. Kit thought he might give up and go below, have a fast, hot shower and get his own dry clothes. Just as he was leaving, she called after him, 'I'd like a Nobel Peace Prize.'

'What for?' Even Kit had heard of the Nobel Prizes, named after a guilty bloke who invented gunpowder. Nothing like aiming for the top award. Peace instead of gunpowder.

'Anything.'

'Don't you have to come up with a discovery or an invention or make things better for others?'

The Great Garbo shrugged. 'Maybe.'

'Have you?'

'No. I just ask the questions. And tell them where they're wrong. I don't have the answers.'

'Doesn't a leader have to provide ways of doing things better?'

'I don't. I'm young.' The Great Garbo twirled her plait end and chewed it thoughtfully, looking up as if to say that made her superior to worriers like Kit.

'You could help Frederick find "how to" YouTube clips about growing seeds on board and solar stuff for making drinkable water.'

GG shrugged. 'Frederick already knows about solar. He likes working things out for himself.'

Then she started a sort-of speech ...

'Like ... other old people have to ask for help for passwords and stuff. So we have the power now 'cos we don't have to unlearn. And we're faster, not because we're younger but we don't have to update, or completely change. The oldies want us to do what they did. Or the way they did it. Because THEY say it. Like ... how they learnt to do something in the olden days. Jobs. Snail mail. Manners. Who needs to know what shank's pony means? But maybe that doesn't work any more. Takes them twice as long. Oldies have to UNLEARN old ways and then learn the new stuff that young people learn first and faster. Like tech. Solar power. Digital. The power balance shifts. We are more powerful ...'

'Unreal.' Kit hadn't thought of power like that before. He was stuck in a bypass. Everybody else seemed to know what to do or how to make things happen. He was just standing, shivering, with borrowed warm gear on the shantyboat deck, longing for a hot shower and his own dry clothes.

Unexpectedly, Frederick slid the panels out to provide shade and store solar power.

Coming up behind them, Steffi commented, 'Not everything is solar or digital. There's spirit power too.'

'Common sense is the best way to solve problems. That's powerful. Like Kit diving in to save Messi. Kit solved that problem. Common sense gets my vote,' Frederick said, adjusting the angle of the panels.

Steffi added, 'And lessons from the lifesaver at the pool, which I organised.'

'And Theo dived in too,' said Kit, surprised by Frederick's praise.

The Great Garbo looked from Frederick to Kit. There was a silence, so Kit admitted, 'I don't know what shank's pony means.'

'Neither do I,' said Frederick.

GG gave a fleeting smile. 'Walking ... to school in the olden days.'

'I walked to school but didn't know it was called that. Thanks, GG, I learnt something new,' Frederick said. 'Now maybe you young ones can help me. I want to find out a bit more about hydroponics ... growing vegetables from seeds on board, but need more fresh water ... and don't have much space ...'

Frederick's hearing was excellent, when he wanted it to be.

The Great Garbo scrolled her device. 'Found you a YouTube animation clip, like a cartoon about growing vegetables from seeds in a small space ... only runs for a minute.'

'Thanks. Don't suppose it's on a boat ...'

'Well, it's really for little kids, but ...'

'That will suit an oldie like me too?' Frederick kept a straight face.

GG smiled, a bit.

'Would you mind if I sketched you later, GG?' That was one skill Kit knew he had.

'Maybe. First, let me see what you've done before. Can I have a look?'

'My notebook is down in the sleeping nook. Good thing it wasn't in my pocket when I dived in to get Messi.'

As they went down the steps, Kit left wet footprints. And he could feel the damp wood underneath his feet. He'd slung his shoes around his neck. But his wet clothing was clammy on his skin. He'd probably picked up a million bugs from that water. He felt shivery. But at least his teeth had stopped chattering.

From the sleep nook, he grabbed some dry clothes. Then he shoved his sketches at the Great Garbo. 'Have a look. I'll go and get changed.'

'Thanks.'

'See you a bit later.'

Was that a mistake? What if she ripped them up? He only had those originals until he scanned copies. He wasn't quite sure if he could trust her.

As she took the sketches away to look at his dried mackerel portrait of Frederick, Kit decided. A frilled-neck lizard, as a show-off. That's how he'd draw her – the Great Garbo with a frill like a face crown. Showy frilled-neck lizard.

He found her in the galley rotating the food supplies, putting the new ones at the back. Frederick had given her that job.

'What do you think?'

'You've got the colours all wrong,' GG said after fingering his sketches.

The Great Garbo was the Princess of Put-Downs.

Kit checked. True. Frederick was not white. He was smoked mackerel browny orange. And Steffi was sort of pink skinned with purple hair this week. Grace's hair was white, but her skin was tawny brown with dark brown lines. Wei Wei was ivory-pearl but ... that's how he saw them.

'Finished sorting the food cupboard. Reckon I'd get a job as an art critic or movie critic next?' The Great Garbo didn't expect an answer.

'Everyone is entitled to their own opinion,' Kit replied. 'Will you let me sketch you now?'

'What?'

'But I only show the subject if I'm happy with the sketch.' Kit was defensive.

Surprised, the Great Garbo sat on the stool. 'Okay. You've got five minutes.'

'Need a bit longer.' He sketched quickly.

'Done? Can I see it? No? I'm off.'

After she left, he put the sketch of her in the recycle bin in the galley. He hadn't captured her. Lizard skin was wrong.

Looking down at his hand, Kit suddenly exclaimed, 'Oh

no!' The Digital Lingo Ringo was no longer on his thumb. Had he lost it in the ocean when he was saving Messi's life?

Now he'd have to own up to Grace, before she noticed.

〰

'What are you drawing?' asked Frederick. 'Interesting design.'

Kit quickly closed his sketch pad. When he drew people the way he saw them, sometimes they got upset. Or criticised him. Like GG. A flag wouldn't complain.

'Designing a flag for *Satellite Freddie*.'

'Just for this boat? What about the other satellite craft? There's a whole fleet of them.'

'Oh. What are the others called?'

'Haven't all got names, as far as I know, a few have numbers.'

'So should I draw a Wasted flag?'

'There's a whole set of rules about how to fly a ship's flag. You're sure to offend someone. Who'd want a flag with rubbish on it?'

'I thought "wasted" meant drunk,' said Kit.

'Got a few other meanings too. Like lost opportunities,' Frederick said. 'Are you going to put it up on the mast yourself? You don't have to climb up to change a flag, you know. Can do it from down here with the ropes.'

'So why did Theo climb up?'

'Ask him. Good excuse. Probably checking on something

else at the same time. Checking on the currents or the type of trash being carried. He's got a few schemes running.'

When you knew you were the King of Clumsy, climbing up a mast was not a brilliant idea. Especially if even superstar athlete Theo had a fall.

'Instead of a flag, adapt the design for something else. Detour it,' advised Frederick. 'Not all ideas work. Sometimes it's better to scrap them. The Wasted flag would need to be legal and there are probably higher priority jobs. We can ask Lex next time – he's the legal bloke, but talk fast because he charges by the minute, even on Zoom.'

'You have to pay to talk to him? Does he have to pay to talk to me?'

'Doesn't work that way in the legal world. He's not a refugee, and you have to pay him. He's part of the new refugee industry. Makes a living out of it. Not like Wei Wei. She believes you donate your skills, not rip off people.'

'I'll go back to cartooning people. Sometimes they can't recognise themselves anyway.' He wished now he hadn't binned that first sketch of GG.

'If you're talking to Mohammed, you might need your ring. Grace did give you one?'

'Yeah.'

'Mohammed is the most popular Muslim name, sort of like "Smith". But they don't all speak the same dialect. Grace said Mohammed was a challenge to record.' Frederick nodded thoughtfully. 'Not sure whether it's better to be unusual or blend in. What do you think?'

Kit shrugged. 'Depends ...'

ZOOM audio recorded and later transcribed by AI for Lex as proof (in case he ever needed it) of how he was persuaded, despite his objections, to work for the Wasted State. (Second copy, for insurance, lodged with the bank in a safety deposit box.) Other voice not identified, but it is female, swallowing the ends of her words.

PERSON X: *Let me tell you a short story. War starts. Your country is overrun. You escape but end up in a refugee camp. You're stateless. You want to work and no-one will have you. You fear your children will grow up as displaced people in camps. Endless forms to fill in via languages you don't understand. Then secretly you hear about a place that is offering shelter. It's legal. Just smelly sometimes. And smoky and unstable but –*

LEX: *Full of leftover activists. They've adapted from protesting on the streets to experimenting with ways to convert the garbage into fuel.*

PERSON X: *We can't save everybody. But if we share a way of doing it, others will copy it.*

LEX: *Trying to get a patent to make money. That's not sharing. It's trading.*

PERSON X: *Face facts. How else will any of us survive? And, Lex, it's in your interest to be our lawyer involved in trading biofuel. You can say it's for climate change, but ... there's a profit for you.*

LEX: *All right. But I'm not going out to that garbage dump, ever.*

PERSON X: *Then you can represent us ... virtually, online.*

LEX: *Let's sort out my percentage first.*

～

9

Real Refugees

'When is my shift?'

'Twenty minutes' time. Before you go, Kit, let me show you something.' Wei Wei's eyes shone with enthusiasm. 'Look at this. Isn't it beautiful?'

The tank on the deck just outside the lab held midnight blue and other coloured jellyfish. They moved and merged into each other as if they were dancing. One was somersaulting.

'Wow.' Kit had never seen such vivid colours before.

'Moon jellyfish are my favourite marine life.'

Kit agreed. They were now his favourites, too. But would he be able to draw them? They morphed so quickly. Maybe painting would work better than pencil. A washy shape in loose brushstrokes. The best thing was he now looked at Wei Wei differently. Wei Wei had shown another side of herself. Previously he thought she was the expert and a bit grumpy. Brilliant, but ... so important that he shouldn't upset her. Now he understood that if she could be so passionate about those beautifully coloured shapes, they might share enthusiasm.

'That's the joy of working in the ocean. And why marine science seduced me. They deserve a water-world that's not littered with plastic.'

'Yeah.' Kit agreed the tank marine world was a bit different from the garbage patch outside. But also the best reason to clean up the ocean. Those clear, pure colours on the shapeshifter jellyfish. Totally awesome ... And no plastic! Would he be able to draw them like they really were?

Kit looked from the deck at the scum of trash swirling in the ocean water. Earlier he had imagined the base would have been firmer, like land, but it was see-through, and the plasticky bits showed.

'So adaptable. Creating their own rafts as the microorganisms hitch a ride and create new worlds of their own.' Wei Wei obviously admired how marine life adapted. 'There's life down there, we just have to give the marine world a chance.'

'Where would jellyfish refugees go? If they couldn't survive in their part of the ocean?'

'They wouldn't. They'd die. That's why we mustn't muck things up from stupidity or greed.'

～

They squeezed into the tiny but busy lab, Frederick, Wei Wei and Kit.

Wei Wei began testing the water quality. 'Our communities

are the blend of life forms thriving on plastic rafts in the middle of the ocean. We've got this mix of species, with some that evolved to be in the open ocean and others that evolved to be coastal, and now they're mixing in this new kind of habitat,' she said enthusiastically. 'I couldn't predict what will happen, but it's fascinating. And as humans we're part of the life forms. We're not victims. We're innovators.'

'How many refugees are there in the world?' Kit was filling the silence. 'Could you guess?'

'Millions. Humans are not the only refugees. Bugs. Insects. Other marine life.'

'They don't all need visas.'

Frederick smiled. 'Most bugs don't have passports either. But they have their own kind of ID.'

Frederick was kneeling like a scrawny grasshopper, with his skinny legs and patched jeans, screwing a handle onto the top drawer.

Glancing sideways, Kit grinned. Maybe he should draw Frederick as a grasshopper, but a smoked mackerel seemed to fit the ocean setting better.

'So how will you get them to live around this garbage dump? Why should they? Isn't it smelly at times?'

'Depends on the weather.'

'And how close you are,' added Frederick.

Distracted by the light filtering through the glass, Kit wondered how he could draw that. Harder even than drawing the exploding colour of fireworks or even explosives. Photographing fireworks was hard. He'd never been close enough to explosives, but Mohammed obviously had. Even when Theo dropped a heavy frypan in the galley, Mohammed dived to the floor. Kit was beginning to notice how often Mohammed overreacted.

'Warzone weary,' Wei Wei explained quietly to Kit.

Dr Wei Wei turned to grab her coffee cup with 'DO IT NOW. IF NOT, WHEN?' printed on it, but it slipped and smashed. Startled, Mohammed reacted again, but this time he left.

Frederick cleaned up the shards, grunting a little as he bent over in the small space.

Wei Wei shrugged. 'Can't solve every war legacy. But my lab rats have worked with me on a way to stabilise then recycle biofuel.'

Kit got it. The satellite boats were just Stage 1. Wei Wei was piloting possibilities. He just didn't want to be one of them.

'Your mother was lucky to get a berth here.'

'And a sleep nook.' Kit realised it might be more comfortable if you were short, like Wei Wei. Not that she seemed to sleep much.

'Steffi thinks she's a social justice activist, but …'

'What's that?'

'A bloody nuisance,' said Lab Rat 1, who had just arrived.

Embarrassed laughter filled the cabin.

Kit felt super embarrassed. Wei Wei ignored that comment.

'This Great Garbage Patch doesn't belong to any country. It's outside the Sea Limits. So it can be a new nation. Legal. But it's unstable.'

'So is your idea.' Wei Wei and Frederick were very different, but they got along well enough to insult each other. A bit different from the GG and Kit.

'Scientifically it's possible to create a base. Using calcification. Building up the atolls, reclaiming beaches, creating new islands.'

'Then what?' Frederick poured water for Wei Wei. He nodded towards Kit. 'Want one before you leave for your shift?'

Kit shook his head. Too much water around him already.

'But they wouldn't all fit. Millions of refugees. Even if you had more shantyboats and islands and –'

'I know that. But we have to start small. Satellite boats are just the beginning. Then coral islands. And buttressed lowlands ... Others can copy us.'

'Who's going to pay for this?'

'Us. Patenting the ideas for recycling as fuel. Every country needs fuel. We're already selling biofuel. And have saved refugees. Got them passports and visas.'

Wei Wei looked hopeful, but only for a moment.

Frederick shrugged. 'And millions waiting. Might be overcrowded, no lifts from the ocean basement.'

'It's just a model. We're proving it here. Ex political activists can be converted.'

'To what? Religion? Messi is ahead of you on that path,' said Frederick.

'No. To use their different ways of thinking to solve scientific problems.'

'Like a growing garbage patch in the middle of the ocean? A garbage dump isn't scientific. It's just leftovers from wasteful societies.'

'Have you got a better idea?'

Kit guessed they'd had this conversation before. They were walking around each other with words.

Theo squeezed into the crammed cabin. 'When I competed under the new refugee flag in the Olympics, they noticed us on TV. Like … that was my contribution.'

'A medal for recycled ego?' Lab Rat 2 suggested, the light reflecting from his shaved head.

'Not funny. I won a Bronze. I showed refugees had potential. Not all were political victims. Then I was invited on the international TV *Survival* show.'

'Did you win that?'

Theo laughed. 'I'm still here. I survived. And we were offered energy sponsorship, which we turned down.'

'But you took the VITA Vitamins sponsorship that paid for the first shantyboats. That was a BIG win.'

Kit hadn't known that. He looked around the tiny lab cabin with the fitted lockers.

'Wei Wei, I've got a question. About the diatoms. Why does Messi say they mean death?'

'What makes you think I've got an answer?'

'Dad said you're the best.'

Wei Wei brushed aside the compliment. Einstein would never have sent him here if he didn't have faith in Wei Wei. Had he known about Cal then?

'Messi twists facts for his own purposes. Diatoms could have unexpected effects if ocean conditions change. And especially if humans contribute to those changes. We need to test. Heard Einstein, your dad, isn't too well again.' Wei Wei dropped discards into the bin. She seemed super cautious about security and safety. How come that cat litter tray got in the lab?

'No, he's not.' Kit kept going with an effort. Einstein wasn't Dad's real name, but a few friends called him that. Dad used to have muscles. Now he had see-through skin and you could work out the bones underneath. Scary stuff. And now Dad was hospitalised. Kit wished he was back home with Dad, but his father had insisted he leave and join the garbage patch shantyboats. No arguing.

'That's why we agreed to Steffi's request for you to live here for a bit. But you've got to do your share.'

'You mean I've got to sort the yucky garbage from the patch. Go out in the boats every day?'

'Get over it. There are kids your age in really bad camps, like jails, on the borders of countries with serious bombing. Some die. "Collateral damage" is what the politicians call them.'

'I know, that's why Mohammed jumps at loud noises.' He'd ask Dad about that the next time he saw him. Dad didn't know Mohammed, but he knew stuff.

Wei Wei continued. 'No clean drinking water. Head lice. Poor food and not much of it. No medical care unless you bribe or pay for it. Tents that leak. Often taken away from their mothers at 12 or 13 and put in with some serious hardcore extremists and terrorists in the adult male section. Steffi was determined to save you from that. We were in Camp 13, one of the slightly better ones.'

'Weren't some of those kids born during civil wars? When their parents were terrorists?'

'Yes.'

'I was with my dad.'

'Yes, your mum made sure of that.'

Kit had always suspected that Steffi just wanted to get rid of him. But maybe that was just a cover ... to keep him safe? So why was he here now?

Kit wasn't sure about his future, with or without ID documents. But he was prepared to do his shifts beside the garbage patch. The food was okay on board. And he knew there was more canned stuff stored in the lockers, which would last for months. But after Wei Wei's talk, he felt almost embarrassed to eat if others didn't have enough. 'I could eat for the Olympics as a contestant' didn't seem the right thing to say now. Not funny.

A voice yelled from outside.

'Kit, you're late. The shift is starting. Go.'

10

Changeover

The deck was busy with the shift changeover. Some people were scrambling down into their canoes and boats. Others were coming on board after hours of gathering samples from the garbage patch. Everyone was carrying sloshy containers. Contents were dumped or poured into a larger container on the deck. The lab rats collected samples. A few workers, like the older men, were quiet. Most seemed to be cheerful companions, as if they enjoyed working together and cracking jokes in different accents. And judging by the bump under their gloves, all of them were wearing a Lingo Ringo. Kit checked. That meant Grace had made lots of rings and maybe replacing one wouldn't be so big a problem, despite her original warning.

Different ages, shapes and heights, plus the babble of lots of languages. Despite their messy work, they seemed to be pleased they were doing something together for a purpose. Or maybe Kit wanted to feel that way because he was heading off soon to do his shift.

That tank of beautifully coloured, moving jellyfish seemed

another world away from the murky depth of the garbage patch ahead. But the memory of it stayed, and Kit wondered whether more beautiful creatures would survive if the Wasted community helped clean up this ocean.

'Here you go.' A worker gave Kit his now-empty containers.

'Thanks. What do I do with them?'

'Take them on your shift. We recycle everything here. You'll find out pretty quickly.'

The changeover crew handed their equipment to the next lot. It was like 'subbing' – substituting a player in a footy match. One person came off and the other went on. Like he remembered at East Beach Primary footy team.

'How will I know what to look for? Or what to collect?' Kit asked. 'Which boat do I go in? Do I have to take my canoe?'

'The *Sardine*? One of the lab rats has already borrowed that to take samples from a specific place. A pick-up.'

For a moment, Kit felt annoyed. The *Sardine* was his. Even if this was a community. 'What's yours is mine.' Was that the way the community felt? Dad always insisted on sharing, but ... they were family.

Since Kit had made it on board, he didn't want to fall in the murky ocean on his way off the shantyboat. Unexpected lifesaving didn't count. The *Sardine* was familiar and comforting and he needed it as a temporary home. Like insurance that he belonged somewhere. His own space.

'Just copy your next-door neighbour when you get out on the water. Wei Wei tells us what she needs from each shift. The boats are a bit like tourist buses – they keep doing circuits to pick up and drop off.'

So Kit did his first shift. At sunset, towards the end of their shift, they switched on the lights on the outside of the shantyboats. It was like a fairyland of lights flickering on the water. Kit separated stuff as asked. It was easy work, as long as he didn't think too much about where the bits had been. And it was good to be part of a boatload of people working together. He listened and learnt others' stories.

'What did you do before?'

'Gardener.'

'Shepherd and goat-herder in off seasons. Herded more goats than sheep.'

'Similar. I was a tourist guide.'

'Trade unionist. Until unions were banned.'

'Student.'

'Cook.'

'Owned a carpet factory.'

'Haircutter. Still got my scissors, so I'll start again, anywhere.'

Some were islanders, displaced when the ocean flooded their low-built homes. A few were sardine fishermen. Or subsistence farmers with too-small peasant holdings. Some older women had the strong hands of manual workers. One was a filmmaker.

'I made a doco of our home in the village. The food and

the festivals and ordinary stuff like kids playing games on the beach. Added a soundtrack of music, voices and local birdlife. My mother watches it when she's feeling sad.'

Kit asked, 'Is it up online?'

Could this be adapted for Wasted in some way? A virtual place? Kit had the curl of an idea that stayed with him. What if ...?

On his return to the brightly lit *Satellite Freddie* hours later, he found a woman bending over tending the deck garden, and Frederick checking the drip system for his new upright seed garden. When the woman turned around, Kit realised he'd met her before, challenging the GG. Bol– ... What was her name?

'How did even one snail get on board and nibble our plants?' she asked no-one in particular.

'Sometimes wildlife stows away on ships, and then leaves when they reach land. Or stays on board, if that's a better option.' Frederick checked the plants. 'I think he has a mate too.' Frederick picked up the second snail.

'Maybe this snail slid on board and was too slow to get off?' suggested Kit.

'Hi. It's hard to remember names at first. I'm Bolour. You're Kit? Steffi's son?'

Kit nodded.

'I know they had problems with cats, rats, mice AND rabbits on the sub-Antarctic islands. Stowaway rats, cats and mice preyed on native land and marine species. Took seven years to eradicate them,' Bolour explained.

'Eradicate?'

'Get rid of. Used toxins of various kinds.'

Kit wasn't sure exactly what a toxin was, but it sounded nasty.

'A toxin is a poison produced within living cells or organisms,' offered Frederick. 'But Kit probably knows that already.'

Kit nodded. 'I didn't, so thanks.'

'Welcome, Kit. Didn't get a chance to say that earlier. The French people eat snails, you know ... with garlic. Frederick has grown too much garlic. Maybe we could use some?'

'I'm not French, B'lour ...' Kit tried to get her name right. At his last school, Kit had been called Git, Kim and Tim. Tim-Tam and even Kit-Kat. So insulting when you were called nothing or the nearest name because the person thought you didn't matter enough to remember.

'It means crystal, in Persian,' Bolour said helpfully. Shaped a bit like a triangle with a small head, medium shoulders and wide hips, her eyes were like traffic markers, super alert. 'When I'm not snail chasing, I'm an interpreter. Sort of a word savant.'

'A memory athlete,' complimented Frederick. 'You have to remember and translate so many words while lots of people keep talking.'

'Thanks. That's praise I'll remember, Frederick.'

She spoke in an approachable way, and her manner set Kit at ease. Some adults are only good at talking to people like themselves. Bolour was one of the others. An older person who spoke to younger ones as though they were interesting and interested. So Kit tried to be.

'Awesome.' Kit was aware of her watching him closely, but in a friendly manner. Did interpreters have to lip-read clues? Or was there another reason? Bolour knew Steffi. And she might have been around long enough to know Dad when he was working as a scientist on secret projects. And the fuss about his early results.

'With a crystal, you can see different angles.' When Bolour smiled, the expression on her face was genuinely interested, not faked. 'It suits my job as an interpreter.'

'In what way?'

'I'm just supposed to repeat exactly what was said but in the language of the listener, and tighten it up a bit. Sometimes you have to be diplomatic. People get upset. Insults are traded. I have to say things with less anger. Refugee camps thrive on rumours. Gossip. The possibility of a visa. A change in government in a country that might accept more.'

'Are you an asylum seeker?'

Bolour shrugged. 'An asylum seeker is just someone trying to find a safe place because their original home is dangerous now. They may have protested. Or been arrested in the wrong place at the wrong time. Or been a relative of someone with the same surname.'

'Or plotted to overthrow the government,' commented Frederick. 'How people describe themselves is up to them.'

'Not always.' Bolour pulled out a couple of weeds. 'Garlic looks strong. Your unofficial herbs might be growing well too, Frederick.'

Frederick shrugged. 'Not mine. But I did hear about some packages floating on the currents and landing near us. Would you know anything about that, Theo?'

Balancing a pile of containers, Theo was climbing down the stairs to their level.

Theo shook his head. 'I'm an athlete. Not an ocean scientist.' He kept restacking the containers so they didn't take up so much deck space. Frederick's tidy habits were rubbing off on Theo.

'Is that your weight training for today, Theo?'

'Lifesaving Messi was enough exercise for this week. Let's check the news first. Before I go on my next shift. Are you going to bed, Kit?'

But something really bad happened next.

〜

The computer screen in the cabin on the deck below was their news centre. *News Flash!* appeared and the audio became louder. The printed news ran across the bottom of the screen.

Young refugee scientist from Wasted community dies from complications. The young woman was originally from Refugee Camp 13, known for its activists.

'How did they find out?'

'Oh no. Not Cal.'

Everyone was upset about the personal loss of Cal. But also that it was on the international news.

'Cal's death is on all the news. I bet Messi the Messiah gave them a tip-off. That's why he came back on his dragon boat. A media moment for him.'

LATE NEWS ITEM

A young lab worker, Cal Smith, has died on the controversial Garbage Patch State. She was working on bioremediation projects on one of the recently acknowledged satellite seacraft circling the new Wasted State. Earlier she had caught Covid, and then was treated with antibiotics for an infection due to a broken arm, but further complications arose. The Great Garbo has been a leading climate activist and the youngest government head of Wasted, now listed in the Guinness Book of Records.

Known originators of this new nation include the internationally known 'Messiah'. And many asylum seekers and refugees, including former Olympic bronze medallist

Theo Yap, who performed under the refugee flag and was the winner of last year's international TV game 'Survival'.

Tomorrow in our Current Affairs program at 7.30 we'll be investigating the issue of refugee visas. And the world of the Garbage Patch State ...

And that's the end of the late news.

Next came a blast of TV commercial music at a much higher volume. The ad was for luxurious tropical island holidays.

'Bad taste in ads,' said Theo.

'Bad news,' Mohammed said quietly. 'Tell Wei Wei now ... that others outside know.'

'Everybody will know soon. Our first death in the Wasted community.'

Mohammed nodded. He seemed to understand without using his Ringo Lingo.

'So many have died on refugee boats. Should have been safe here.'

'Short-lived utopia,' said Bolour grimly. 'This was meant to be a good place.'

A very worried Wei Wei appeared at the cabin door.

'I wanted to keep this news about Cal private,' said Wei Wei. 'Who told the media?'

Wei Wei looked around the cabin at the shocked faces.

'We didn't.'

'Not me.'

'Why should we?'

Kit wondered why Wei Wei's name was not mentioned on the news. And where the news channel got the photo so quickly. Kit had never seen Cal's face before. But her photo had filled the screen. Blonde, 20-ish, with alert, sparkly eyes. A sparrow tatt with a name on her shoulder, which Kit tried to read sideways and couldn't.

'So beautiful.'

'So vital.'

'A hard worker.'

'Kind girl. Thoughtful.'

'I'll finish her tests,' Lab Rat 2 offered. 'Promise.'

'That might not be a good idea. Let's wait until we find the real cause of her death,' said Wei Wei, looking around just as Messi swept into the cabin. 'That may have international consequences.'

Wei Wei was keeping it official, but there was grief in her eyes. She fished out another tissue, but then, 'God's will,' pronounced Messi.

'How do YOU know that?' Wei Wei was outraged that Messi trivialised and appropriated news that had such significance for the Wasted community. Cal had been her responsibility. Those trauma tourists brought Covid and she got it. And then Cal had antibiotics for the infection from her broken arm, which may have caused complications. 'No, not God's will, I gave her the antibiotics,' refuted Wei Wei. 'But it could happen to others. We must retest everything.'

'And how long will that take?'

'As long as we need to be sure.'

'Months? Years? Forever?'

'We'll find out the facts. As long as it takes.'

'What if we don't retest? Why not apply for the patent but keep the testing going at the same time?' Messi suggested.

'Can't do that. We need proof that the bioremediation works. That the calcification can mend the coral atolls and provide a base to live on. Otherwise there's no patent.'

'Remember there's two separate patents: one for the calcification and one for the biofuel. If Wasted's reputation is affected, that will stop trading in both. We need the biofuel payments to survive. The advances won't keep us going for long.'

The mood in the cabin had shifted. From shock at Cal's death to fear and wanting to blame others. Everything changed with Cal's unexpected death. And the possible causes. Kit wasn't quite sure when the sympathy for Cal turned into fear on the *Satellite Freddie*, but for some of the crew it did so instantly, and there was quiet muttering all around the cabin.

'If Cal got sick from working in the lab ... will it happen to us too?'

'Do you think it's something from handling all the trash?'

'But we've been so careful with bio-security.'

'Gloves. Masks.'

'Cal's death might have been caused by something else.'

'Such a big shock. Especially to Wei Wei who had been working with her for … how long?'

'Since the beginning.'

'Who else was here in the beginning? Are they at risk too?'

'I was,' said Bolour. 'And Frederick, and his partner Max. It was their boat, which they'd already sailed around the world in. But then they decided to anchor here.'

'And Cal?'

'Cal was an orphan. She turned 20 on the shantyboat. Remember we had a bit of a party? With all those candles and Frederick was worried the boat would catch fire?'

'Who could forget that. The gift-wrap paper did catch fire. But we put it out.'

Wei Wei looked thoughtful but still sad. 'Cal was young and fit, but after Covid and anti-viral treatment, her arm broke in a trivial fall, and she had antibiotics for the infection. Novel complications arose. That could have been a sign that something else was wrong. The calcification project might have side effects for humans.'

'You need calcium for your bones. But only the right amount.'

'Especially for those with continuing exposure in the lab. Maybe the after-effects of the antibiotics she was prescribed had a toxic effect.'

'What?'

'We need to find out.'

'How long before it might affect us?' asked the lab rat. 'Or are we safe?'

No-one wanted to answer that. Or maybe they didn't know. But it could have implications for at-risk people in the future. Whatever had happened to Cal could perhaps happen to them. That was the fear.

Kit wondered if Dad might have some solutions. But it wasn't fair to ask Dad when he wasn't well himself. Should Kit ignore his father's request and go back regardless? It had only been a day since he left, but ... Kit couldn't really ask Steffi what to do. His mother wasn't good in real emergencies, only made-up ones, with her at the centre of the drama.

Time to sleep. So much had happened.

⌇

11

Cal Consequences

Wei Wei's Thoughts, Recorded

I've decided to record my testing notes on this project, in case anything happens to me. I'll use a notebook and an audio recording back-up. The lab rats can continue if necessary.

I was so focused on pitching patents for the bioremediation, I didn't think about the impact on my assistants like Cal. I was just trying to solve the scientific challenge and get it right. Find the answers. And retest for sure. A young girl has lost her life because of exposure. To my research ... or lack of it. Did the calcification project exposure affect Cal's health? Were her bones affected? Was that the reason for the broken arm in such a young person? It's possible. Covid plus a reaction to antibiotics and a novel toxin? I just want to find answers. And if it were released in the ocean, who else would die? Instead of using calcification to build up atolls as fake islands and legal states, by releasing it into the ocean might I affect the bio-balance of other lives? Human and marine.

I can't bring Cal back, but I can find out why she died. What really caused her death? Other scientists have had suspicions that antibiotics might occasionally have adverse effects if coupled with other, earlier issues. Long Covid is an unknown. So is calcification. We're in unknown territory but there's no time to waste.

I'm investigating in the lab every minute possible. I don't want another medical tragedy. So much risk in bio-experiments. People are complex. There's a comfort in the patterned structure of the biological world. It's there, but humans don't always realise. Until a label is given to a virus or a disease or a cure, we're working blind. But I MUST find out what caused her death.

Einstein's the only scientist who might understand or be able to help. But he's out of range. I can't ring him or even email. I can't even have an imaginary conversation so I can get my head straight.

But I know what he'd ask: 'Why are you working on calcification?'

My original answer would have been: 'To build a base to extend our islands and atolls.'

'Why do the toxins worry you in Cal's case?'

I know toxins can bio-accumulate in diatom predators

like mussels and scallops. Later these may be eaten by higher predators (like humans?). These unknowingly ingest lethal phycotoxins. But Cal never ate fish!

⌒

Lab Rat 1 opened the lab door.

'Wei Wei, I've been listening to you talking to yourself. Are you sure you're okay? There's no-one else here except me.'

Lab Rat 1 came closer. It was touching that an assistant really cared that his boss might be losing it. Kindness? Or more that he was worried about his future?

'I'm trying to work out answers to Cal's death.'

'D'you think it's a toxin?'

'Because a toxin is protein made by a microorganism, it interacts with human cells to cause adverse effects – like the tetanus toxin causes severe ongoing muscle contraction and another toxin causes severe diarrhoea.'

Lab Rat 1's face was serious. 'These algae poisons can cause illness, epilepsy, paralysis or death in the unlucky victim. I didn't know that before. Look, Wei Wei, I found this.' He read out his notes, *'The first linked deaths were three elderly people who ingested contaminated mussels in 1987. Periodic detection of these toxins has closed fisheries.'*

'What if I play devil's advocate and ask the awkward questions?' Wei Wei suggested.

Lab Rat 1 nodded.

'What if a novel toxin could occur from novel diatoms? This could cause gastrointestinal disease with malabsorption (this leads to osteoporosis) and could lead to death.'

Lab Rat 1 looked blank. 'I don't know.'

'Neither do I, yet. That's why we have to keep asking questions.' Wei Wei kept going. 'Are we messing up the bio-balance while creating a legal state? On the forever scale, maybe visas don't matter.'

⌇

Wei Wei kept audio recording, just in case her notes might help others solve the mystery later.

So complex! The halophilic bacterium provides a carbon source and other nutrients essential for all living processes. In the waters around and below, fish colonise the area and grow rapidly, fed by the diatoms. That was early in our research. But now...'

⌇

Wei Wei stood back from the screen, looking very worried. Should she share her decision with the other lab rat and with Lex, or do more tests first? Could she stop the patent process NOW? Should she? It was just a suspicion, not yet proof. If this had contributed to Cal's death, there was no way she would agree to submitting the patent to release anything into the oceans. It didn't matter how much money was being offered, nor the pressures from Lex, nor the refugees they'd be able to fund.

She had to say no.

It would not be a popular decision. It would destroy the dream of a utopia. Bolour would have a reason for challenging her. And maybe a takeover as Head of State. If Messi didn't get in first.

～

'If we stop the patent, we will have nothing to trade. No income,' said Bolour.

'You're right. But it could be a temporary measure. We just need more time to retest to make sure it's safe,' Wei Wei said.

'What about those Swiss bank accounts Lex mentioned that are holding Wasted money?' Bolour was relentless in her attack. 'Existing patent royalties? They'll stop. This will destroy our Wasted brand. Our reputation for climate repair solutions.'

'Probably,' Wei Wei admitted.

Bolour's face was setting in determination. 'What about the refugees?'

'All the money from the sale of our patents is used directly for the refugees. Isn't it?' Frustrated, Wei Wei tugged at her twist of hair, which fell around her face, revealing white at the roots as well as strands of silver in the black.

Bolour shrugged. 'Except what Messi and Lex manage to

skim off the top. The Great Garbo wouldn't have a clue about spreadsheets and payments.'

'You don't have proof. Just suspicions.'

'Messi ran an advertising agency for non-profits ... never made a profit because he scammed them. That's why he had to leave his country. He's a criminal, not a refugee. Check who signed the documents. I bet Messi has his name on the financials.'

Bolour paused for a moment, then continued, 'One email would be enough to destroy international trade. And the Wasted community would have no bargaining power once they lost the ability to trade their climate solutions. Messi will be dead against you retesting and destroying the Wasted brand.'

'What about those millions affected if we release a toxin into the ocean?'

That was the decider. Wei Wei went into action. No was harder to say than yes.

⟿

On deck, the morning wind was fresh. It was between shifts, so those on board who were awake early were clearing and cleaning the decks. So much to look after. Plants. Machinery. Ropes. Sails. Repainting. Moving solar panels. Checking the generator.

Bolour twisted a scarf around her hair so it didn't fall down into the piles they were sorting. The Great Garbo was watching but not helping much. She was twirling her plaits again. Just one of her nervous habits. She also bit her fingernails, or what was left of them, Kit had noticed.

Kit glanced across to the darker Great Garbage Patch, where it was thickest with debris. Weird that they were cleaning the deck and out there was all the trash other people had dumped from boats, hotels and cities. You'd expect water to be clean, but this ocean was polluted, unlike the well-scrubbed boat deck. On board they recycled just about everything. Out there it was a floating mess, like trash soup.

That dirty ocean must annoy Frederick, who was conducting his own clean-it-up campaign. His tiny, clean shantyboat against the rest. A private protest.

'You missed a bit here, Kit. Give it another go with the brush.'

Would it be difficult to have an ocean burial out there? Kit wondered. Bolour looked up suddenly.

'Burials do occur at sea,' she said.

'But sort of tacky to mention it,' added the Great Garbo. 'With Cal on our minds. She's on the mainland now. Her body, I mean.'

Could they read his mind? Kit had suspicions about the Lingo Ringo's hidden powers. Or did they both need to be wearing the ring? He wasn't. He'd lost his in the murky ocean. One way only. If Bolour and GG could still read his mind, then there was some digital link he didn't know about. Or they were just good at reading people.

Changing the subject, Kit asked, 'Does the Digital Lingo Ringo have a find-your-ring function?' This is what he needed to know now. But he also added, as a distraction, 'Or a swearing function?'

'Check your own.'

'I can't.'

Bolour was offhand as if thinking of more important subjects. 'Probably, I haven't checked recently. Grace added extras after she asked for my professional content. Wanted samples when she developed the prototype.'

'You mean I could swear in all languages?'

'Why would you?'

Kit shrugged. Bolour had a point. Swearing was boring because most people said 'f—' instead of 'very'. All the time. But some thought it meant you were part of that group. And they needed to belong. Using their own special words kept others as outsiders. Kit was usually an outsider, so he observed a lot. In some of his cartoons he used speech balloons, so if he added swear words, would his work be banned? Might mean more people looked at his work, but ...

'Do you use the Digital Lingo Ringo?'

'I've been a professional interpreter for years. How can an app do as good a job as me? Why would I want to put myself out of business?'

The Great Garbo had been quiet for at least a minute. That was unusual. Then her long, stretched sleeves flapped as she pointed overboard. She asked, 'Kit, if your Lingo Ringo is down there, seeing you LOST it, in the ocean … do you think marine creatures are using it to talk to each other in fishspeak?'

Surprised, they all laughed.

Bolour answered semi-seriously, 'No, because when one of the early Lingo Ringos fell down the latrine toilet, Grace had to make a new one.'

'Because it wasn't waterproof? Or it was too smelly? Or too hard to get back?'

'Dunno.'

'Perhaps fish just guess each other's thoughts?' suggested Kit. 'By the way they move?'

GG interjected, 'Being an interpreter is just a word channel. Like a streaming service. You pay for words and if you don't like their service, you replace them. Interpreters will be replaced now. Your sunset industry job will be gone, like LP records and CDs.'

'What's a sunset industry? Sounds beautiful.' Kit imagined a sun ball sinking in the brilliant red, tawny orange and bright yellow rays of a sunset, going down into the dark and how he might draw shadows with purple-grey.

'Jobs that don't exist any more. Found better ways of doing them. Like … analogue recording technologies … like … for audio or video. All gone. All digital now.'

Kit looked at the Great Garbo's face. She was saying exactly what she thought. Was that bad manners or honesty?

Wasn't the Head of State meant to be diplomatic, or was that another way of opting out? Or lying? Or using lots of words to say nothing?

Meanwhile Bolour frowned as she realised this 'streaming' comment was an insult to her. But was it intentional? Was the Great Garbo challenging her mentor? Kit watched as Bolour struggled to mask her real reactions to the Great Garbo's unfiltered comments. And the fear that the interpreting skill Bolour had would no longer be valued. She'd have no skills to sell. That was a real worry, whether it was called a sunset industry or having no job. No role. No status …

'I don't need you any more, Bolour. I've outgrown you. I don't want to listen to what you think. I've heard it all before … You just repeat yourself.'

'Yes, I repeat myself. Maybe because you weren't listening.' Bolour's face wasn't professionally neutral any more. She was seriously annoyed. And the frown line between her eyes had deepened.

'Why should I? Everyone wants my opinion. I'm the Great Garbo. You gave me the title and the job.'

'Opinion without proof isn't wisdom. Being a critic or complaining is easier. You don't have to deliver workable solutions. Now your real job is to keep everybody working together. Especially after a tragedy like the loss of Cal.'

Bolour left, her feet thudding on the deck.

Kit wasn't sure. Was Bolour trying to help? Kit didn't want

anyone controlling him either. Fair enough, Bolour might feel a bit fed up that the digital ring was taking some of her interpreting work. Or that she'd helped the Great Garbo, who took her skills and all the credit for her work. But ...

'I liked Cal,' admitted the Great Garbo. 'She wasn't jealous. She just wanted to find answers to climate stuff. And work in Wei Wei's lab. And she always asked me how I was getting on and listened. She knew I was a bit different.'

'Nothing wrong with being different,' said Kit. 'All my family are.'

'If you're so different from your family, does that make you the same as some other people? Maybe you just have to find the different-different people?'

For the first time, they laughed together, not AT each other. Then Frederick suggested they get back to work. 'Finish the first coat on the outside of the wheelhouse. Only take 15 minutes with two of you. Brushes and paint there.'

'Let's do some different-different painting,' said GG.

So they took the paintbrushes before Frederick told them off for slacking.

'Brunhilda was a warrior queen. I googled her,' Kit admitted. 'From Norse legends.'

'Still don't like the name.'

'Me neither. How about I just call you GG?'

'Okay.'

'Do you know the names of any famous artists?'

'Kit?'

They both laughed.

'Let's do it together.'

'Okay.'

'Different colours? Faces?'

Then they took it in turns to add some paint to each.

Later, Frederick wasn't keen on the funny 'different' faces they'd painted on the wheelhouse. 'Just graffiti!'

So they repainted the faces and made them into fish.

And signed 'Kit/GG' as the artists.

⌐

Shouting voices in the corridor. One booming voice was familiar.

'Let me in.'

Messi forced his way into the galley; his bulging tummy arrived first, taking all the spare space. Bolour and the Great Garbo were stuck in front of the oven griller, imprisoned by the agitated Messi, whose hair stuck out as if an electric shock had been switched on. His beard was so bushy he looked like a leftover Father Christmas gone to the dark side.

'I want to talk to Wei Wei. What's this about stopping the calcification patent?'

'Wei Wei isn't here. We're just making a snack. Want a cheese toastie? Or a pizza slice? Or a home-grown shantyboat salad with tomatoes, chillies and –?'

'No.' Messi was erupting. 'Where is Wei Wei?'

'She's not here. This galley isn't big enough to hide in. Try her lab.'

'Wei Wei is not the only one who can speak for the Wasted community. What about our Head of State? Shouldn't her digital signature be on any documents?' suggested Bolour.

By 'her', who did Bolour mean? Kit thought GG had already chucked that job. Did Bolour mean herself as a replacement?

Messi's eyes lit up and he fronted the Great Garbo. 'Did you digitally sign anything recently for Lex, as Head of State?'

'I just gave the job away a little while ago.' The Great Garbo turned to make herself a hot chocolate with double spoonfuls. The steam curled up from the mug with 'The Great GG' on it.

'Latest news,' commented Theo.

'What? How can you do that?' Messi was breathing hard.

'I just did.'

Bolour collapsed on the only stool in the galley. There was a smell of burnt toast, so Kit turned off the griller and pulled out the smoking, cheesy mess.

'Want me to scrape off the burnt bits?' he asked.

'Forget it,' Bolour said.

The Great Garbo tipped the burnt toastie into the recycling food bin. The she started making a fresh one for Bolour. 'I'm good at toasties.'

'Burnt toasties again?' someone muttered. 'Thought that was Theo's specialty.'

'Finding the truth about Cal's death is a more important issue. Other financial or Wasted decisions need to be postponed, for the moment.'

'Wei Wei's name is on the patent application. Permanently.'

'What if she dies? Or isn't ... er ... well enough to sign?'

'She'll be replaced.'

'Who by?'

'That is the million-dollar question.'

Messi stormed out of the galley.

'Toastie's ready, Bolour,' offered GG.

'Someone else can have it.'

Kit wondered if she meant the job or the toastie.

12

Spy Cat

That cat was a mistake. But whose mistake? You couldn't control a cat. They were aloof and looked down on humans. They did exactly what they wished, ate when it suited and sometimes allowed humans to serve them.

Kit couldn't understand why someone as fussy as Wei Wei would put up with a ship's cat like Shadow in her tiny lab.

'How do you feel about cats, Theo?'

'Prefer big cats like Bengal tigers or lions, but they wouldn't fit in around here.'

'Ever noticed anything special about Shadow?'

'Bloody nuisance. Useless ship's cat. Never caught a mouse in its life. Especially since the kittens arrived. Always escaping onto the deck. Shadow follows them. That's the reason Wei Wei is paranoid about shutting the lab door.'

'About Shadow's collar. Notice anything special about it?'

Theo shrugged. 'A bit over the top for a cat. More like jewellery than a collar.'

'It's a body-cam.'

'Really? I should have looked more closely. You're right. Why put a body-cam on a cat? It's not as though the cat can tell us where she's been.'

'Has the camera been there all the time? Is Wei Wei keen on cats?' asked Kit.

'Not especially. Not as keen as Steffi with dolphins.'

Kit tried to smile. His mother was always embarrassing.

Had the cat always had a body-cam and nobody noticed? Or was it a recent addition, since the loss of Cal?

Was it to monitor crew or Wei Wei's results in the lab? Who was looking at the footage? Where was the footage? Did Grace have access? Why not just ask her?

So Kit did, in a roundabout way.

The galley was the best place for a gossip and finding out stuff. The usual smell of burnt cooking lingered after Theo left. Grace was having a salad in the galley and Kit took his mug to her bench table.

'Okay if I join you?'

'Of course.'

'Grace, you know how traffic police on the mainland now have head-cams to collect details about accidents ...'

'We don't have police on Wasted.'

'But there's a body-cam on Shadow.' Kit paused. 'Do you know who put it there? And who collects the footage? Do you have access to it?'

'So you noticed? You're the first one to mention it.'

'You did ask me to tell you if I noticed any cameras.'

'True.'

Kit gulped his hot drink to fill the pause. He spluttered as it went down the wrong way.

'Too hot?' Grace queried and thumped him on the back.

Kit shook his head, coughing. 'I'm okay.'

Concerned, Grace watched him. He hoped she wouldn't try that anti-choking technique where you grab the patient around the back. He'd learnt that at first aid too and was worried that someday he might need to use it.

'Ah.' Kit was breathing properly now. That was a relief. Why did things always go wrong when he needed to ask important questions? Was it just anxiety that made him stuff up? Did she think he was rude to ask her directly about the body-cam?

Was it someone not on board? Messi? Lex the lawyer? Or maybe more than one person, working together? Who needed to know if the bioremediation fuel really worked? Or listen to conversations? Would someone be checking progress in Wei Wei's notes?

'Did you want to ask me something, Kit?'

His brain seemed to be working again even though his mouth felt scalded. Luckily she seemed more approachable than he anticipated. And she could only say no.

'Was it your idea to set up the body-cam, Grace?'

'Lex asked me,' admitted Grace. 'Easy enough to set up.

Hardest part was getting hold of the damn cat.' Grace showed him the scratch on her wrist.

She seemed to be a secretive person usually, but was willing to talk to him now. Was it because he'd proved he was observant? Or had other things changed? Like Cal's death?

'I've never met Lex, but I know he's the lawyer. Isn't it illegal to record if the subject doesn't know?'

Grace smiled. 'As far as I know, cats can't take you to court.'

'Shadow the cat isn't being recorded. Wei Wei or the lab rats might be.'

'True. You've made a good point.'

Kit wasn't giving up. 'Why didn't you have a fixed camera in the lab? The cat was just carrying the body-cam and moving a lot.'

'Yes. And it roamed all over the ship and recorded a few conversations. But mainly in the lab. Lots of frustrating interruptions when the cat moved before the end of some human chats. Background noise. Or didn't keep her head still long enough to read anything.'

'If the cat moved her head, did the sound drop off?'

'Yes.'

That meant Grace had listened to the audio. Was there more than one copy? Had Grace sent the cat-cam file on to Lex? Why did it matter?

'What were you listening for?'

'Lex wanted surveillance to check on the testing progress. If it would be safe to go ahead.'

'Couldn't he just ask Wei Wei?'

'Sorry, got to go now.' Grace stood up. 'We'll talk about this another time.'

Kit hadn't found out enough about Lex yet. He'd try again. Dad always said never give up. Or maybe he should warn Wei Wei about the body-cam. But now, when she was so upset about Cal, was not the best time. Grace hadn't answered the question about why she didn't set up a fixed camera. Had she wanted it to fail? And not give Lex all the spying information he wanted?

〜

In the lower decks, the sleep nooks were tightly placed in small spaces. Kit remembered Wei Wei's suggestion about 'weighing' people. Maybe it was a benefit to have small people, but that was unfair to broad Mohammed whose weight was a strength for some jobs. He hoped Mohammed managed to sleep in his cramped space with his stocky body. Worse for Theo, who was longer. Maybe Theo could have a double sleep nook?

Mohammed didn't say much but he listened and worked quietly, often with Frederick if the task was a two-man job.

'Refugees work hard or give up in despair. Mohammed is a worker. That's why the boss chose him,' Frederick said. 'He used to help Cal by carrying down the samples for the lab.'

The Great Garbo appeared. 'Do we need to pack up Cal's things?'

Bolour nodded. As a newcomer, Kit felt a bit in the way. He and Cal had never met, but she sounded like someone he would have liked as a friend.

Cal's name was still on the sleep nook. Carefully Bolour peeled off the name and packed up Cal's belongings. The Great Garbo folded Cal's clothes, and Bolour took down the photos of crew life on board. That was sad. Cal didn't have family photos. Kit knew his photo was in Dad's wallet.

'Cal's name will still be on the tent Steffi was showing us.'

'We won't let Messi claim credit for that too.'

'What else did Messi claim credit for?'

Bolour shrugged. 'Everything possible. He believed that if he said lies loudly and often enough, people would believe him.'

'Such as?'

'Wasted was his idea. And he developed it for the international market. Not true. Not like Cal, who was modest. You would have liked her. Everybody did,' Bolour said. 'But if she'd suffered from complications due to exposure in the lab, her death may be serious for others too. Might stop the whole project.'

'Wei Wei tell you that?'

'Wei Wei was worried about calcification affecting humans if it were released into the oceans. But she cared about Cal personally too. Sort of like a daughter.'

WASTED?

The Great Garbo listened intently. 'I wasn't that interested in the scientific stuff. I just knew Wei Wei was creating a new utopia. But things went wrong. Messi went psycho. And we lost Cal.'

'Messi attracts lost souls, especially low-esteem females or vulnerable males who become followers,' explained Bolour. 'I'm not one of them. Neither was Cal.'

Kit had wondered why his mum was here. Although she was excellent at making short-term friends. But then they disappeared, like Rangi, if he ever existed in the first place.

'Have you got your Digital Lingo Ringo, Kit? I want to check something.'

'Er ... no.'

'You'll have to go and see Grace.' The Great Garbo shrugged. 'Tell her what happened.'

'She'll think I'm an idiot.'

'Probably.'

'I won't be able to get another one.'

'I'll share mine if that happens.'

'Rent a Ringo? What will that cost me?'

'My mum used to say, "Worse things happen at sea."'

'NOW? We're in the middle of an ocean.'

Both laughed.

Sounded like the Great Garbo wasn't close to her family. Kit felt the need to stick up for his family.

'Dad and I get along okay. Steffi and I are different.'

'So I noticed.'

Kit was proud that Dad stuck up for things he believed in, including Kit.

'Okay, GG?' said Kit

'Gee Gee sounds like a horse.'

'Yeah.'

'I like watching horses gallop. I've never ridden a horse, but ...'

'Only seahorses out here.' Kit gestured towards the bluey-grey waves, which were increasing. White lacy frills on the top. Not dead plastic this time. 'That's what Steffi called the waves when I was little. Seahorses.'

'Cute.'

'Not when you're a teenager.'

'Heard about the sneakers?' GG asked Kit.

'Yeah.'

'Some idiot lost or dumped sneakers overboard. So scientists tracked the plastics on GPS or they put markers on them to check where they've come from. The climate worriers got really worried. About other marine debris too. Made a kind of spinning mass of water called gyres. Now we've got garbage patches. Bit of a worry. Micro particles in an area twice the size of Australia.'

Kit thought she MUST be exaggerating. But sometimes she surprised him. GG knew more scientific stuff than he thought she did.

'Most strangers don't know we're here, yet. Refugees get directions. But even Google Maps have mistakes in remote places. Tracks that don't exist. Or unmapped islands. Soon we'll be a world power, Wei Wei says. Others will use our ideas and have a place to call home.'

Time to face Grace. After their body-cam cat talk, Kit wasn't sure he'd be welcome. He followed the others across the deck and knocked on the wall next to Grace's space.

'Excuse me, Grace.'

Grace's reaction was unexpected. Immediately she held out another ring. 'Catch this. Heard you rescued Messi. So I'll forgive you just this once for losing your Ringo.'

Kit was stunned. He was ready to tell the truth.

'I'm not sure if I lost it lifesaving Messi. It might have been –'

'I know. If you lose this one, no replacement.'

Waiting outside, Frederick winked at Kit as he left. 'Now there's a turn-up.'

'Thanks, Frederick.'

How did Frederick really feel about all the new arrivals like him? Originally it was Frederick's private space on the water, which he had built across the years, and suddenly all these extra people were arriving. Plus the dragon boat rowers, but they were temporary and most had left by now.

But how could you say no to any asylum seeker who had nowhere to live?

'Did you prefer living alone out here, Frederick?'

'At first, my partner and I built the very basic raft and then kept adding to it. We enjoyed the adventure. Just the two of us.'

'What happened next?'

'Some journalist wrote a feature about us. And took photos. Then a doco on YouTube. That's what Bolour and Wei Wei saw, which gave them the idea for the refugees and the Wasted State.'

'A YouTube doco! Cool.'

'Not really. Allowing that doco was my mistake. I was proud of my tiny cabin carpentry. Wanted to show it off.' Frederick looked regretful. 'Lots of solo sailors document their journeys and sell their stories. Max, my partner, didn't like the publicity that followed. Not everybody wants to be recognised. We'd been living very quietly before. Then people from his past found him. So he just vanished again. I haven't seen him since. Miss him.'

'Oh.' Kit fiddled with his replacement ring. It seemed a little different from the earlier one. Did it have other powers?

'Adventurers often build their own vessels and sail for a season or forever. Some are sailing to adventure. Others are running away from their past mistakes.'

'Don't you need money to set up on the water? Like to buy food and stuff?'

'Yes. Building or renovating a boat takes lots of time and money. But you learn survival skills while you're doing it. I met one bloke who built his boat in his front driveway over about five years, but then it was too big to get out. Had to get a crane. His wife was ready to divorce him. He fell in love with the boat-to-be and left her.'

'He divorced her for a boat?'

'Some break up for less.' Frederick smoothed his hand along his woodwork.

Kit wasn't sure why his parents broke up.

Frederick continued. 'If you're crossing the ocean later, and something major goes wrong, at least you've got some idea if you crafted the original. Even if you can't fix it alone. Most sailors go out of their way to help others in distress. Weather is the big challenge, especially storms, but also the local politics sometimes. A few dangerous pirates out there.'

'Pirates!' Kit imagined a skull and crossbones flag.

'No. The modern pirates are mainland rebels seeking hostages. Blackmailers. Some boats sink. Weather has to be respected.'

'Is that why you're always checking?'

'Of course. And some refugee boats vanish. Overloaded in bad weather. People smugglers only care about the upfront dollars.'

'Anything good about being out here?'

'Some wealthy explorers pay boat builders to fix things

and take the credit, but others are like us. Making do with a fixer-upper. Risk-takers "crew" for them just for the ride and visit ports and places you'd never have a chance to see otherwise. Beautiful bays and islands. Heaven. Better than the photos and movies.'

'Did you have crew?'

'Just Max. He was a good navigator. You need that to find your way home. But for several years he was "inside", so his navigation skills were a bit out of practice.'

'What was he in …' Kit stopped his question.

'In prison for? Fraud. Insider trading. He was better with money than me.'

Kit changed the subject quickly. Maybe Max wasn't better with money if he ended up in jail.

'Can you do that … sky stuff … navigation? Could you teach me?'

'Celestial navigation? Yes. Mohammed knows it better than me. He's an experienced sailor too.'

'Wow.'

'That's the old way of navigating by the stars. Everyone has to learn today's navigation devices and how to keep the vessel going. Most travellers are legitimate but a few are involved in dodgy deals or running away. Best not to ask too many questions about what they did before. Just listen to their version of their history. Tall-story tellers most of them.'

'Ever had to rescue anyone?'

'It's expected that you help each other.'

'Is that why you said yes to Wei Wei and Bolour?'

'Not at first.'

⌒

The Great Garbage DRUG PATCH. Kit started sketching on his pad. Ideas were easier to explain in shapes. Instead of black lines and shading, this time he used blue. He enjoyed exaggerating and adding comical bits. Currents like a giant washing machine. Carrying stuff in little white packages with fins on. The fins were an extra. But they could swim in the same general direction each time, if you waited long enough for the circular motion of the current. He drew a map of continents and islands within a washing machine. For fun, he added a box of liquid cleaner to cleanse the ocean washing machine, but then deleted it.

Kit looked out across the opaque water. What if that current was more than a rotating sea of plastic? What if it really was a transport system? If so, who was using it? And what about pirates? Water thieves? Or worse?

Kit's brain pictured things. That's why he had to explain things slowly, in idea stages. Show them in a diagram. Or others would think he was weird.

They'd probably still think he was weird anyway.

Was it possible to rely on regular currents to deliver packages? Drones were quicker but had to pass Customs and Quarantine. Who could he ask that had the scientific knowledge? And who wasn't already using those currents illegally. And was an experienced marine scientist. Would one of the lab rats know and be willing to explain? Or should he just try Dr Google? Theo had been checking something when he climbed the mast, before he fell. Was he involved? But as an athlete, would he become involved with drugs? He was proud of being super fit. Wei Wei was the best to ask, because she knew the most about everything, but would she be furious if smugglers were taking over her patch? Or pirates? How would you know the difference?

Kit sketched a tiny jellyfish in sneakers in the corner. His new signature.

～

'The ocean currents might bring more than garbage you know,' the Great Garbo said.

'What do you mean?'

'Theo told me there are drug routes too. They lose a few packages, but the drug smugglers know where the ocean currents are likely to go. Send them off from one continent and arrange to pick them up later from another. Lose a few in between.'

Kit decided to check.

'Excuse me, Wei Wei. What if something else drifted with

the waste ... like following the currents? Would smugglers know the route and where the packages would end up?'

'Yes, Kit. An experienced marine scientist would know enough about the tides. And how long it might take for something to float to a destination.'

'Someone like you?' suggested the Great Garbo.

'NO!' Wei Wei turned on the Great Garbo. 'That's a drug washing scheme. Why would I RISK the good name of our Wasted community? It would affect trading our patents. And our potential income to support refugees. Only a fool would do that.'

'Sorry,' Kit fiddled with the testing stuff on the bench, sort of tidying up, but the Great Garbo kept putting things back. She whispered, 'Leave it. Wei Wei likes things done her way ...'

Wei Wei turned. 'Yes, I do.'

Kit shrugged. He was only trying to help.

Had Wei Wei suspected the marine smuggling route for some time? But did she suspect anyone on board? Which fool? Or had he got it all wrong? Was someone negotiating with the smugglers for a percentage? Allowing a bit for wastage and things floating in the wrong direction. Was Messi already 'skimming' what he considered his share? From the drug currents?

But then the Great Garbo played with the idea as if she owned it. 'The Great Drug Patch? In the State of Wasted? Sounds a clever idea.'

Kit wished she'd shut up.

'Not on my patch!'

Disgusted, Wei Wei left but GG kept talking, 'If Wei Wei didn't go ahead with the diatom distribution, and international states didn't pay to trade, Messi couldn't "skim off" what he considered was his share. Maybe drug currents are his insurance. Another way of getting money.'

'Any proof?' asked Kit.

'Who needs proof?' GG raised her eyebrows and left.

Kit screwed up his sketch and threw it in the recycle bin.

⌒

Kit was sitting on deck, balancing his pad on his knees and sketching quickly. He expected to be given another recycling job any minute and he wanted to capture his idea first.

'What are you drawing?' the Great Garbo asked.

Kit shrugged. 'An underwater cartoon. You can look if you like.' He was still annoyed with GG for blaming others without proof. She didn't seem to notice how she affected people with her outbursts. Gossip and facts weren't the same.

Once she'd said something, for her it had gone, but her comments stayed with others and hurt.

He offered her the pad. She turned it around. Then upside down. Kit wasn't sure whether she was really interested or just being irritating.

'Looks like coral in outer space. How can you draw what's underneath if you can't see it?'

'I'm outlining the coral and I'll let others fill in the colours. Sort of choose-your-own-future. What might happen if the coral is badly affected and goes toxic.'

'Which colours?'

'Anxiety Blue, Emergency Red, Extinction Orange. Night Black. Bleach White. Greenwash Green and Danger Yellow … I know that doesn't start with Y.'

'Awesome,' said GG. 'A cartoon warning. How about Yucky Yellow? Or Doom Dark Brown? Or Trashy Tangerine …? I could share that in my next climate dangers interview.'

Frederick overheard. 'It's Kit's idea, not yours. Like the seekers' patent was Wei Wei's idea, not Messi's. And this boat was originally mine. Some of us would like to be acknowledged for our work.' He hammered at a stray nail sticking out on the deck.

'But if we share the ideas, more people will use them.' The Great Garbo didn't like criticism. Kit had noticed that. She usually attacked as a way of defending herself. She did it again now.

'You can't use that Black word, Kit. It's an insult.'

'It's a colour. Black. If something is black, why can't you say it's black? We've had this colour conversation before,' Kit reminded her. 'When I was telling you about my creature caricatures.'

'Sorry, I forgot.' The Great Garbo looked at the skin on Frederick's muscled arms.

'Yes, Frederick is smoked mackerel browny orange.'

'That's not an insult, it's a fact,' corrected Frederick. 'The colour's from working on board in the sun. What colours did he use for you, GG?'

'All of them. A frilled-neck lizard, with lots of colours. The Great Garbo with a frill like a face crown. A showy frilled-necked lizard.'

'Got that right,' laughed Frederick. 'It's a compliment when an artist draws you.'

Kit heard the word 'artist' as if it were on loudspeaker. Nobody had called him that before.

'Have a closer look, GG.'

With Frederick's encouragement, the Great Garbo looked more closely at Kit's sketch.

'Is it a sort of climate change cartoon? What's this in the corner? Looks like sneakers?'

'Well, I heard about the dumped sneakers.'

'Looks like a jellyfish in sneakers.'

'Why not?' said Kit defensively. 'It's my new signature.'

'Sorry. Your mum taught me to weave and to knit, but I haven't drawn much.'

'And what about the ropes? You were good at knotting them,' said Frederick.

'You reckon?' The GG was pleased. 'You said you'd teach me to use that sextant after I learnt the ropes.'

'Have you got your own sextant?' asked Kit. 'What is it exactly?'

'Belongs to the boat. If you want to learn about celestial navigation, we need a sextant. It's a nautical tool. Measures the angle between two objects viewed by its optical sight. Works out where you are. We've got one below. Maybe tomorrow I'll show you.' Frederick pulled out his binoculars. 'Or ask Mohammed if he's got time. He was a fisherman years ago. He knows more than you'd think.'

Kit sat beside Frederick, looking up at the speck in the sky.

'Are you seabird watching, Frederick?'

'Sort of.'

'Is it a bird? No, it's a drone,' said Kit.

'Wonder who's paying for that. And what's in the drop?' GG said.

'Official business for Wei Wei?' suggested Kit.

'I just deliver to the person on the label. They paid the delivery costs. It's their business,' Frederick said.

Hesitantly Kit knocked on the closed lab door. It slid open. The inside catch dangled with a clink.

'You told me not to come back unless I had a good idea.'

'I meant it.'

'When I was with Dad, we played a few games on screen. Virtual reality stuff.'

'So? Get to the point, Kit. Or put these old results folders away on the top shelf for me while you're thinking. May as well use the time.'

This shantyboat was full of people telling others to tidy up. Like a feeling that if they didn't use all the time they had, something bad would happen. It wasn't just about climate change repair. It was like they were fending off DOOM by keeping busy.

'Maybe it's a bit of a weird idea.' Kit paused, stretching to the top shelf.

'Tell me, then I'll tell YOU what I think of your idea.'

'Nobody wants to live on a rubbish dump.'

'That's not news. We all know that. But it's just part of the process: bioremediation, getting a patent, trading with ideas and being part of a geographic state, becoming legal. I know that's complicated for a newcomer, but we've been working on this for so long now. And have to keep explaining to people who don't think like us.'

'But what if we made a virtual reality place of Wasted? Can I show you this?'

Kit held up his device and Pacific Islands music and voices played. 'These islanders were recording their island before it went under water. Wanted to save their culture. Virtual reality. See the clip.'

'Yes.' Wei Wei watched.

'When I was on that shift to the garbage patch, one of the islanders alongside told me about his beaches and coral atolls vanishing into the ocean. Gave me an idea.'

Wei Wei was getting impatient. 'So ... nice music but ...'

'Rising sea levels and awesome storms are forcing islanders to leave. So someone had the brainwave. Make a virtual reality film. Sort of how the place used to be. Put it on YouTube. Limited access.'

'Nostalgic. But what's the use of that?'

'What if ...' Kit paused. 'What if you offered refugees a virtual passport, so they didn't have to come here to the garbage patch. It'd be sort of legal ... Tied to the virtual state. Recording something that wasn't there any more. As a sort of comfort to those who needed a ... what's that word for something you inherit?'

'Legacy?'

'Yeah.' Kit wished he'd sketched it. His ideas were stuck in cotton-woolly clouds ... and he didn't have the right words ready. He hadn't quite worked it all out yet and he knew Wei Wei demanded logical stuff. All he had was a vague idea ... but maybe she could fit it up and make it work.

'How do they earn it? Do they pay for it? Just watching a YouTube doco isn't enough. And why would they want a video of the ugly garbage patch? We want to get rid of the waste.'

Kit thought. 'I know it's not a beautiful Pacific island, but ... maybe they want to remember working here ...'

'They already do that.'

'And then their family get the digital code on their mobile for their passport and visa.'

Wei Wei wasn't convinced.

'Like ... I went through the airport with my dad a few years ago. You show your ticket and like ... everything is on your phone.'

Wei's Wei's face was thoughtful. 'Kit, you might have the atom of an idea here ...'

'What's that mean?'

'I'll let you know.'

'Okay. Like ... Theo might know more about recording. He won that TV *Survival* game, the international one. They filmed him a lot. And, viewers watch the reruns all over the world. Even in Antarctica, Theo said.'

'Leave it with me, Kit. Go and help somewhere else. Try the comms cabin. Check how things run there,' Wei Wei ordered.

～

WASTED?

Wei Wei's Thoughts, Recorded

Kit seemed the usual time-wasting, clumsy adolescent whose overused word was 'like'. With Steffi as a mother, he didn't get much of a start.

But his dad, Einstein, taught him to ask questions. A very intelligent man who wasn't afraid to make a stand on his scientific experiments, AND had the patience to follow things through. Such a waste that he is now in palliative care.

I must learn patience ... and try to listen to questions from youth like Kit, even if he rambles. Luckily Grace is digitally skilled enough to play with this idea and make it work. She's already proved that. And I can rely on Frederick, even if he's a digital dinosaur.

∽

On the deck, Wei Wei said, 'Look out for that drone, Frederick. Important evidence on board addressed to me. I can trust you. I needed to check the tests I did on Cal with an independent laboratory. That doesn't come through online and is more detailed.'

'No worries, Wei Wei.'

The worry persisted. No-one wanted to be known only as the doctor who lost patients and offered misguided hope to refugees. And certainly not as the boss of a crew member who might be smuggling something illegal via the currents.

Like all the cabins, the comms area was cramped. Lights glowed and warning sounds beeped. Kit wondered if he'd learn how to operate all the screens and understand what the maps, graphs and gauges meant. If you messed up, crew on board had to fix it. This was an isolated world that had to be self-sufficient. Was that why Wei Wei sent him here to learn from Theo and Bolour?

Theo handed a printout to Bolour.

'Can you translate Cal's medical report, Bolour? Into words we can understand?' Theo asked.

'Gastrointestinal means it's in your gut.' Bolour flicked through the report. 'Mal means bad or not working properly.'

'Anything to do with the MALdives? Great holiday place,' Theo offered.

'No. Malabsorption is imperfect absorption of food material by the small intestine. Osteoporosis means trouble with your bones. Anything cardio is to do with your heart. Toxicity means poisonous: "the toxicity of a drug depends on its dosage". A toxin is protein made by a microorganism that interacts with human cells to cause adverse effects ...' Bolour paused. 'Okay that's the end of Medicine 101,' she said.

'That sounded really complicated. Big words that mean it was super dangerous,' Kit said.

'And you're in real trouble if all that's wrong with you!' Bolour commented.

'Like Cal. And maybe others in the future?'

The cabin went quiet.

'Green tea, anyone? It's calming,' offered Steffi. Her special teapot was on a tray with matching cups. Those delicate Asian decorated cups with no handles.

'No thanks. I prefer your seaweed patties,' Theo said.

'Ran out. But I'll make more tomorrow.'

'No ... er ... you'll be too busy with the Cal tents,' Theo added quickly.

Steffi smiled. 'No problem.'

'Last time the tea was so hot, I dropped the cup, the tea went everywhere and the china shattered,' admitted Theo. 'I felt bad about that. Sorry, Steffi. Better not to trust me with your special cups. So I'll give the green tea a miss thanks, Steffi.'

Rejected, Steffi said, 'Wei Wei drinks my tea when she's working late at night in the lab. She says it's calming. I often leave a thermos for her.'

'Your turn to mop the corridor, Kit. Bucket and mop here,' Theo said.

⏤

In the corridor, as Theo and others questioned Bolour, Kit listened as he cleaned the floor, giving it a last mop-over. Some people stepped gingerly around him, avoiding the still-damp bits.

'Did Wei Wei know? That other medicos were concerned about bad reactions with a novel toxin after antibiotics?' said Theo.

'Yes. That's why she feels so guilty now. She cares,' said an unfamiliar voice.

'A lot of refugees died in the camps. And others earlier on the boats. Wei Wei used to help everybody,' Bolour recalled.

'But she lost that royal bloke who belonged to the ruling party, didn't she?' Theo added.

'What went wrong?' someone asked. Kit didn't recognise that voice.

'It wasn't quite like that,' Bolour began. 'But she wasn't able to save that patient ... the son of one of the important families who were overthrown. And they have long memories.'

'What happened?' asked the deep voice belonging to the person Kit couldn't see.

'Just a really risky operation. "Do it or else" ... Only skilled doctor ... Wei Wei was forced to operate for political reasons. Then he died and she was blamed. Now she's trying to find an answer to Cal's death,' Bolour explained.

'For Cal's sake? Or the sake of the Wasted community? Or for her reputation?'

Kit squeezed the mop into the bucket. Now there were footprints all over the floor. So much cleaning to do on board and out there in the ocean was more stuff to tackle. How about a giant vacuum cleaner in the sky to suck up all the plastic pollution? Reverse cycle of the water bombing during bushfires. He could draw that later.

Meanwhile, it was a waste of time mopping this corridor with all of them tramping out of the comms cabin and sharing their worries about Wei Wei's decisions.

⌇

Later, the shantyboat was quiet and dark, although the outside lights were on, and the rocking was getting worse from the increasing height of the waves. Most people on board were sleeping after their shifts, but for those awake, moving in the passageways was difficult as the boat rocked more violently from an approaching storm.

'Be careful. We don't want any broken bones from falls. Hang on to the railings,' cautioned a crew member as he passed.

Holding the thermos, Steffi tapped on the lab door. Then tried to jiggle it open. The door was closed with the inside latch on. Was someone working inside? It was well known that Wei Wei worked late in the lab, alone, and drank her green tea last thing at night. Eventually Steffi gave up, took the thermos back with her and went to her sleep nook. After her night podcast talking about the Cal tent, she was tired anyway.

⌇

NEWS

Dr Wei Wei was found unconscious in her lab on board the shantyboat 'Satellite Freddie'. She is in a coma and unable to answer any questions.

～

It was a dark and stormy night, just like in the beginning of most mysteries written by AI. Noise from the rocking shantyboat would have covered any cries for help.

'Who found her?'

'How did they get through the door?'

Frederick was upset. 'There's a latch on the inside. And the door just slides, usually, but she'd fallen and her weight was against it. We jemmied the door open. Well, I did. Steffi was with me.'

'Why would someone want to put Wei Wei out of action?'

'What happened?'

'Not sure. Somehow she fell and hit her head on the bench. Maybe, due to the storm, chemicals spilled and produced toxic fumes that Wei Wei inhaled. Or someone hit her deliberately. She's in a coma. She was taken by speedboat to the mainland hospital.'

'Who found her?'

'Frederick.'

Bolour looked thoughtful. 'Really sad news. But there have

been documented cases of scientists being poisoned by non-traceable poisons.'

'Accidentally? Or on purpose?'

'Scientists know more about non-traceable poisons than most. But Wei Wei wasn't going to poison herself.'

'No proof she was poisoned, yet.'

'Not the green tea then? With poison added?'

'Unlikely.'

'I took the thermos back with me, but she had cold leftovers from the previous night.' Steffi was very upset at the accusation. 'Are you saying the green tea might have been poisoned?'

'No, it probably just tasted revolting as usual,' said GG.

'My mum wouldn't do that. She admired Wei Wei,' Kit said.

'Oh!' Steffi seemed grateful that Kit defended her. 'Wei Wei is the only one who likes ... liked ... my special tea. I made her a thermos most nights.'

'It's better than Steffi's seaweed cakes,' muttered GG. 'But not much. I'd rather have hot chocolate.'

Kit smiled slightly.

'So somehow Wei Wei fell and hit her head on the bench? Or was pushed? Or fell over something?'

Kit was thoughtful. 'What about the body-cam on the cat? Wouldn't that have recorded her fall? Was the cat looking at her? Or even in the lab?'

'What body-cam?' quizzed GG. 'I've never noticed it.'

'On Shadow's collar.'

GG was thoughtful. 'A cat would look towards a noise. So the camera should have been pointing that way.'

'Who has the footage?'

'Maybe it's still on the cat?'

～

'There's Shadow. Up on the ledge.'

'Move slowly. Don't startle her.'

The cat leapt skilfully from ledge to bench and peered down disdainfully at the humans below.

'*Miaow.*'

'She's laughing at us.'

'Is the body-cam still attached?'

'Yes. On her collar. She's probably filming us.'

'Whoever watches this will get a shock. The Great Cat Chase.'

'Portholes are shut!' GG checked. That cat might fit through an open porthole, but they couldn't.

Quickly Kit slid shut the cabin door. That reduced the number of places where Shadow could escape.

'You move in from that side, GG. I'll come in the other way.'

Two humans in a small space. And one agile cat.

GG lunged and missed, just as Kit grabbed at Shadow. They fell over each other, giggling.

Shadow was off again. Over the screen, skidding on the table and landing in the hammock before scrabbling up the sleep nook bag. Then, with a flying leap, squeezing through the sliding door just as Mohammed opened it from the outside.

'What's happening here?' Mohammed grabbed the cat and held Shadow firmly like a baby with its legs dangling.

~

Kit put the body-cam footage into the laptop in the cabin.

It was murky, at times very dark, and it was hard to make out anything. Lots of cat noises when he turned up the volume.

GG looked over his shoulder.

'Is that a teacup on the bench?'

'Yes.'

'It doesn't mean your mum is a poisoner. She just makes awful seaweed patties, and green tea is not everybody's favourite drink. Probably Wei Wei was re-using some from the night before and couldn't tell the difference. Iced tea.'

'Yeah.'

Kit suddenly went on alert. Steffi was the only one likely to be blamed for the green tea. Had his mother been in there earlier with Wei Wei? He needed to look at all the footage first.

'What's that? Is it a crack in the lens?'

'A cat's whisker?'

A couple of test tubes had been knocked over.

The small body on the floor was in shadow against the door, entwined with the fallen stool. White coat. Dark hair in a ponytail. Blood on her head.

'And there's Wei Wei's arm and her notebook.'

Was the notebook still in the lab afterwards? Would it have her latest test results? Where was the notebook now?

⌇

'If Lex organised the body-cam on Shadow … like … to monitor test results, who else has a copy?' GG asked. 'If Lex needed to go ahead with the patent, big money was involved.'

'Dunno.' Kit had never met Lex and wasn't sure he wanted to. But Kit was trying to understand. Would knocking out Wei Wei stop the retesting? Cal's death might already affect the Wasted brand. And if Lex couldn't get money for the patent … was that a motive? Why remove the scientist who was likely to make money for you? Even if she had said no until further testing.

Mohammed had been listening closely. 'Do we go back to work now and do our shifts …?'

So they did.

It was Frederick who had organised the Medivac boat to take Wei Wei to the mainland.

'She'll be safer there,' he said.

Safer from what? thought Kit. Certain people? Infection? And where was her notebook?

⌇

178

13

On Trial

UN Investigation into an incident on board *Satellite Freddie*. Zoom conducted by Pan.

Via a Zoom screen on a satellite boat beside the Great Garbage Patch, they were now part of the investigation, on trial: the whole Wasted community.

Pan had demanded an earlier visual tour of the shantyboat's galley and lab as potential crime scenes. Taking the camera, Frederick proudly opened and closed drawers and revealed the ingenious foldaway larder in the galley. Oats, flour, coffee, spices and healthy stuff like green tea in recycled see-through containers. Yeast for bread making.

Solar panels and a garden on the roof. Like a hobby farm on the sea.

Then the cramped cabins and sleep nooks. Lastly the lab.

'Thank you, that's enough,' said Pan. 'We're not tourists being entertained on a webcam. We are now investigating the scene of a possible crime.'

～

The comms hub of *Satellite Freddie* was crowded. And other satellite boat communities were linked in.

'Is that United Nations symbol real or is it a fake setting?' came a loud voice from the back.

'Shh. We're not on mute,' Grace cautioned, flicking controls. Setting up this enquiry had been technologically challenging. Grace was busy adding names and roles under screenshots, her end, to make the Wasted community look more professional.

'Why do we need an outsider to investigate?'

'Because we are all suspects.'

A face appeared on centre screen, with the UN logo behind.

'Let me introduce myself. I'm Pan. Since you are in the Away State and there is no security force or police, I'm the UN Authority. I'm investigating this serious incident on board.

'Dr Wei Wei was found unconscious in her lab on board the shantyboat *Satellite Freddie*, Wednesday at midnight. No-one had seen her since 8 pm local time. She's now in a coma in a mainland hospital and unable to answer any questions.

'Each of you will be interviewed by me, in turn. This will be recorded.'

Pan had a deep, tawny voice, like an experienced Shakespearean actor. 'Who is in charge? Where is the Head of State?'

There was an awkward silence, which wasn't a technical

malfunction. Then Grace spoke. She was looking a bit strained, like most event organisers covering up likely incompetence by participants.

'At the beginning of the start-up, we didn't have one. But we needed a name others would recognise internationally. So, the Great Garbo was given the job. As a very young and passionate climate change activist, she attracted attention.'

'Not always the right kind,' someone muttered.

'I'm the Great Garbo, I was the first Wasted Head of State.' She pulled the hoodie back from her face. 'But ... sort of ... an ex now.'

Bolour interjected, 'I'm standing in for the Head of State, just for your investigation into Wei Wei's accident. I've known her longest. I'm Bolour, the interpreter. I was with Wei Wei in Camp 13 when the Wasted community was started.'

'Explain your role on the boat,' instructed Pan, whose face was neutral.

'Asylum seeker, skilled, stateless and in need of a visa. Best if I give you some background first –'

'No,' Pan commanded. 'Just answer my question.'

Bolour looked a bit annoyed at that order, but lifted her chin and continued.

'The *Satellite Freddie* raft was Wei Wei's test case to provide a stable base near the garbage patch. Could a community make a living from bio-recycling, especially biofuel? And if it worked for the first craft, how quickly could they add more craft and more refugees? They needed to be able to trade internationally. That's why the asylum seekers with special skills were so important.

'The aim was to add more people as space became available and their skills were needed. And Pan, your UN has acknowledged the Great Garbage Patch as an Away State.'

'True. But what if they didn't have any scientific skills? Some refugees were illiterate peasants.'

'But all were the type to persist. Highly motivated. They'd already survived extreme hardship.'

Everybody nodded agreement.

Pan said, 'Just facts, not opinions, please.'

Bolour continued. 'Everybody was worried. If you're a refugee, you're likely to be anxious, because change has happened so fast. Adapt or die. Maybe you don't have the skills to work on the raft. But you need a visa and the Wasted State could issue one. Wasted offered hope.'

Pan repeated, 'Explain your role on the boat.'

Bolour protested that she was trying to explain the context.

'Should only relevantly skilled asylum seekers be invited? In George Orwell's *Animal Farm*, all animals are equal but by the end some are more equal than others.'

'Not relevant,' said Pan.

'Haven't read *Animal Farm*. Is there a film?' muttered Theo in the background.

'Yes. An animation too,' whispered Grace off-screen.

'Asylum seekers and refugees are not necessarily the same groups ... and every asylum seeker family has political baggage. Not all get along. May have been on opposite sides during uprisings. This was meant to be a safe haven. Not like some of those islands, the ones governments use for detention, internment or prisons.'

Theo interrupted. 'There are tropical holiday islands too. Aren't they places people WANT to go?'

'Not relevant. Don't interrupt,' said Pan.

'Half the Pacific tropical islanders have been forced by climate flooding to move ... Wei Wei negotiated some contracts about that. And climate-refugees are relocating to us, with a fee paid by governments.'

Pan nodded. 'I require you to answer my questions in order. State your name. Your role on the boat. Your relationship to Dr Wei Wei. And where you were when she was attacked, or fell. How long have you been a refugee or asylum seeker? What are your skills?'

'Sounds like a job interview form,' was a background mutter. As Grace changed the microphone volume controls, Theo interjected.

'You want alphabetical order? If not, I'll go first. I'm Theo.'

'What is your full name?'

'Theo Yap.'

Theo held up his Olympic medal, and his refugee flag was draped across his muscled shoulders like a cape. The light was at a flattering angle on the best side of his face and reflected the medal. He'd probably practised earlier.

'I'm Theo, the Olympic athlete. If I hadn't participated in the Olympics under the refugee flag, no-one would even have heard of this place. Of course, I wasn't the only refugee athlete to compete. Later, the reality TV show helped with media exposure. Luckily, I was strong enough to survive the mountain climbing and the wilderness, and that program showed internationally. Bolour saw it.'

'What was your role on this boat?'

'Grunt work. Wei Wei was looking for more "muscle" to build and extend the satellite rafts. Frederick was already in place. But I was also a refugee in search of a visa.'

This UN investigator had global experience in egos, but stuck to the questions. 'Your relationship with Dr Wei Wei?'

Theo nodded. 'She said I was eye candy and she was on a protein diet. Didn't get that. But I'm the sort of "muscles" poster model for "grunt work". Then the garbage patch community needed more scientific knowledge.'

'To do what?' Pan questioned. 'Specifically?'

'Turn trash into something useful like biofuel.'

'And?'

'To patent it and make a living. And attract more trade.'

'Explain the trade link,' instructed Pan.

Theo looked a bit blank so Bolour moved centre screen.

'Wei Wei said not to look at the garbage as trash. Look

at what it might be. Bio-mass that can improve lives. Like medicine. Or fuel. Or building materials. At first we thought this could be a safe place ... a haven. Despite the smell and the ... possible infections. Any place has problems. Wei Wei suggested the rafts as satellite labs. We had to start small.'

Pan insisted, 'Can we stick to the order of the questions. Theo, where were you when Dr Wei Wei collapsed or was attacked?

'When was that?'

'Wednesday night between 8 pm and midnight. In her lab, with a latched door.'

'I was asleep on deck until they woke me up, because I had an early shift. I sleep whenever I can because it's a bit cramped in my sleep nook.'

'How long have you been a refugee? What are your skills?'

'I've been a refugee since before the last Olympics.'

'How many years have you been a refugee?'

'Seven years. Others have been much longer.'

'True,' muttered Messi. And because he spoke, the main screen flicked to Messi's face. 'My turn.'

Conscious he had lost centre screen, Theo kept talking. Grace fixed that. Messi's face vanished and Theo reappeared.

'It's not like a luxury cruise being next to a marine rubbish dump. I'm okay with a physical challenge and I'm single. But if I had a family, would I worry about the toddlers falling overboard? Or getting sick? Of course. But then Wei Wei talked to me. Or she talked to my chest because she's so tiny and I'm taller than average. I remember the conversation. "Theo, I want you to do something for me, for us."

'"Anything, Wei Wei," I said. I admired that woman even if others are a bit scared of her. She has so many brain cells, she's out of my league.'

Pan: 'Relevance of your answer to the question?'

'Originally, I was prepared to do anything to compete in the Olympics. Bolour contacted me because I used to be a long-distance swimmer and didn't need any expensive equipment. The refugees didn't have the resources, but I could still march under the refugee flag.'

'That's correct,' Bolour said. 'You only needed bathers for that. Or swimmers or cossies or costumes. Same stuff, different names in different states.'

Pan: 'What are your skills?'

Theo looked puzzled. 'Depends who's asking. I'm adaptable. Can do most things. But never drugs.'

'Thank you, Theo,' said Pan. 'Could we hear from Bolour again please? I'm aware Bolour's name has a special meaning. Suits an interpreter. In Persian, a crystal has many facets and it all depends upon the angle from which you look.'

Kit poked Grace. 'Sounds like a Wikipedia entry.'

Grace nodded.

Her parents wouldn't have known Bolour was going to be an interpreter. What if they'd called her … Kit couldn't think of a name bad enough. His name meant everything, '... the whole kit and caboodle'. At least they hadn't called him cavoodle, like a poodle-cross dog. And luckily he wasn't called Grace, being so clumsy.

Pan focused on Bolour.

'What are your skills?'

'My skills are interpreting. And translating.' Bolour's answers were getting shorter. Probably super experienced with bureaucrats. Or shortening others' words.

'How did you gain your language skills?'

'Lived in refugee camps when I was young and had a good ear for languages. But I wasn't a third culture kid.'

'What is your definition of that?'

'Born in one culture and living at home in another and maybe schooled in a third, but your parents could also come from other cultures.'

'So?'

'My parents weren't around.'

'Where were they?'

'Heroes of the revolution.'

'What's that mean?'

'Executed as collaborators in the uprising.'

'Were they?'

'No, but they had no chance to write their version of history later. Or put it on social media. Just a label.'

'Should we call you an adult of a third culture?'

Was Pan trying to put people at ease or just getting a definition for future use in a database?

Bolour answered, 'Your choice. Not an accurate description for me. I'm a survivor of many cultures. I didn't always get to school in the camps. They kept grabbing me to translate … That's when I learnt that the interpreter can influence events. Just put a bit of a spin on it.'

Kit whispered, 'Spin or lie? What if others overhear and know both languages?'

The others heard but ignored Kit.

'Did you think of yourself as an asylum seeker?'

'I worked out which skills were needed to get out of the transit camps and seek asylum. Whoever was in charge needed interpreters because they couldn't run the place if no-one understood what they said. You must be aware of that, sir.'

Kit watched Bolour closely.

'I could tell them what to say. "Feel good" words. Which words to avoid. Like … democracy. Has a million different meanings, depending on who is using it and when.'

'D'you ever get words wrong?'

'Maybe.'

'Does anyone know?'

'Probably not.'

'Anyone complain?'

Bolour shrugged. 'Hard to prove.'

'What is your understanding of "asylum"?'

'A safe place. A seeker is a person trying to find that safe place. Nothing worse than feeling you don't belong anywhere and that there's no hope of change. Even a garbage dump where you can prove you are not political rubbish or collateral damage. That's a start.'

Pan: 'The official definition is that "an asylum seeker is someone trying to find a safe place from their original home which is dangerous because of political or religious intolerance."'

'That fits me. And most of the others on board.'

'What was your role? Why did you come to the garbage raft, Bolour?' Pan was back in official investigator mode.

'I was in Camp 13 with Wei Wei when our visas were turned down, again. Together, we thought of a start-up. This was after years of waiting on the legal lists and getting fed up when other refugees queue-jumped for various reasons.'

'Genuine natural disasters or political fraud?' Pan was very precise.

'Both. Effect was the same on us. The Garbage Patch State was our last-chance idea. We knew it would be tough, but it took longer than we expected.

'Living ON the garbage wasn't an option. Fire and infection danger. And we needed to trade bio-recycling in some way. But look at what's happened now with the bioremediation and calcification. The implications of Cal's situation are terrifying.'

'Hence I'm conducting an inquiry,' said Pan.

Hence? Who used an old word like that? Kit gave up. This was just another adult word ramble. They weren't going to do anything to fix the problems.

Pan ordered, 'Steffi Mayo next. State your name. Your role on the boat. Your relationship to Dr Wei Wei. And where you were during the time she might have been attacked.'

'Steffi Mayo, recycle designer,' said Steffi proudly. 'And eco-influencer. Designer from recycled materials. I've designed and made fittings for the sleep areas of the shantyboat. And emergency tents for refugee camps.'

Before Steffi could go on Pan said, 'Your data also states that you are a tea ceremony host. Could Dr Wei Wei have been affected by something in her nightly ritual of drinking green tea that you gave her?'

'No.' Steffi was definite. 'I didn't leave fresh tea that night. Her door was latched.'

A few people around the screens on other satellite boats muttered, as this was news. Many had not known the details of Wei Wei's collapse.

'How long have you been a refugee?'

'Since I lost my passport, was caught in a warzone and ended up in Camp 13, where I met Wei Wei and Bolour.'

'Where were you on Wednesday night?'

'On the shantyboat. Making extra snooze-bags because my son Kit had joined us. Also did an online podcast interview, so I can prove the time I was talking. There'd be a recording with time codes.

'But I did find her unconscious when I returned with Frederick to check on her at midnight. We jemmied open the door. Or Frederick did. I was gutted. But it wasn't my fault she collapsed.'

Pan said, 'Thank you. Now I will interview Kit, Frederick and Messi. And Grace. I also have Mohammed and Lex on my list, but they are not here.'

Grace nudged Kit, who unmuted his audio.

Kit said, 'My name is Kit. Steffi Mayo is my mother and I have to live with her now because my dad is sick. Dr Wei Wei thought I was super clumsy.

'I was watching the footy online with Frederick while we sorted recycled stuff. Then I went to bed. I used to be listed on my parents' passports, but ...

'My only skill is drawing cartoon people, like animals or marine life. So I notice things, like you seem to be –'

Pan interrupted, 'That's enough. Frederick next.'

'My name is Frederick Schmidt. I designed the original shantyboat from recycled materials. I had experience in living off-grid with my former partner. Dr Wei Wei invited me for my building skills.

'Between 8 pm and midnight Wednesday, I was streaming the international footy final. I do have a passport. I forced the latched lab door when we were worried about Wei Wei. Steffi was with me.'

Pan commanded, 'Messi next.'

Messi eagerly took centre screen. 'My name is Messi, which is short for the Messiah. Religion is my trade. My role on the boat? Yet to be arranged.

'Dr Wei Wei and I disagreed over secret bank deposit boxes and where patent royalties should be used. Also over WHEN I should be Head of State.

'My skills are arousing mob support for Wasted as a new nation.'

Pan tapped a comment onto his device. 'Grace next. She's the digital expert who invented that translation improvement?'

Steffi interrupted, but Grace put her on mute.

Pan's voice dominated. 'Unmute yourself, Grace. What is your role on the boat?'

Grace answered crisply, 'The Digital Lingo Ringo. And the function of simultaneous translation to enable refugees to communicate across the satellite vessels.'

Pan queried, 'Could you design a function to translate or program thoughts and memories?'

Grace looked surprised. 'That's a very advanced concept.'

Pan: 'Answer the question.'

Grace: 'Yes.'

Pan: 'Do you and Steffi share skills? Anything in common?'

Grace: 'No. Steffi claims she is clairvoyant and intuitive ... but this Wasted project is digital and scientific. Entirely different.'

Pan: 'What was your relationship with Dr Wei Wei? Any disagreements?'

Grace was exasperated. 'Wei Wei was trying to build a safe economic future for refugees. A new utopia. No more war. She was ethical. She traded scientific ideas. But she wasn't prepared to risk contaminating oceans and killing millions of people until her ideas were properly tested. Others were. So they "nobbled" her. She was in the way of them selling the bioremediation for big money.'

Pan: 'Who is "them"?'

Grace: 'That's your job to find out.'

Pan: 'Where were you when she was attacked or collapsed?'

Grace: 'On board, working.'

Pan: 'How long have you been a refugee?'

Grace: 'About 20 years with no visa. Stateless. I'm an asylum seeker because of my earlier political involvement.'

Pan: 'What are your skills?'

Grace: 'Here? Digitally linking all the satellite boats. Designing digital devices to be patented to earn income for the Wasted community. An awareness of the use of bots. In simple terms, bots are computers pretending to be human. AI. Artificial intelligence. But they can be programmed to hack, spread misinformation, steal data and –'

Pan: 'Can a bot kill?'

Grace: 'Yes. But only by certain means.'

Pan: 'Examples?'

Grace: 'Not relevant to share here. Eco-industrial espionage is a problem.'

Pan: 'And ...'

Grace: 'Pan, I think you are a bot. I refuse to be questioned and condemned by AI.'

There was a sudden uproar in the cabin. Everybody surrounded Grace, who flicked the mute button, and then 'LEAVE' and the screen went blank.

Everyone spoke at once, crowding Grace for answers.

'Grace, could we switch back,' requested Kit earnestly. 'So I can ask a test question?'

Pan reappeared.

'Pan, what is the question you LEAST want me to ask. And what is your answer?' asked Kit.

MALFUNCTION appeared on the screen.

'I'll refer that to our UN committee,' said Pan.

'Who had the MALFUNCTION?' someone asked.

'It depends on who controls the bot,' said Kit. 'That's why I asked that test question.'

'The one who sent a bot to judge us?'

'Probably another AI.'

'But who is the human behind them?'

'The million-dollar question.'

Bolour suddenly realised something. 'Lex wasn't interviewed by the bot. Why not?'

'Duh. Because he wasn't on board,' offered GG. 'Pan didn't get to Mohammed either, but he doesn't answer officials on most subjects.'

'Lex doesn't come here, only contacts us online.'

'Maybe Lex organised the Pan investigation?'

'Or Wei Wei's accident or whatever happened,' muttered someone in the background.

'Why?'

'Money. Trading will drop off. Existing patents will be affected if we withdraw on this one.'

'Do you think Lex set up Shadow's body-cam earlier to check test results?'

Exasperated, Theo took over the floor, his strong legs wide apart.

'That's a stupid idea! You can't control where a cat will go! Shadow isn't going to stand in front of notes so you can read them on the web security screen. As far as I know, that cat can't read. Or be able to be in the right place to photograph and experiment. Lex probably wouldn't care what the results were. He'd just want to trade them. And Grace knows a cat is unreliable as a security camera.'

Talking about a cat seemed less tragic than Wei Wei's coma.

So suddenly the cabin was full of energetic suggestions. 'To watch lab results ... so he'd know test results first?'

'Monitoring Wei Wei?'

'I agree. Lex is more likely to worry that Wei Wei would do endless tests and he wouldn't get his percentage. So much for utopia!'

Bolour looked thoughtful. 'Lex had other clients besides

us. The Pacific Islands group. I know he talked to them ... the Prime Minister and the politicians. Especially the Minister for Trade. Big money involved. I had to do some Zoom interpreting for them. They had recently signed ocean bed mining licences around their islands ... for minerals and whatever else was down there. That would contaminate the ocean for sure.'

'Why didn't the Prime Minister use the Digital Ringo Lingo?'

'This was a while ago ... before Wasted patented it. Lex checks future investments. He's probably got a real estate licence for Mars! And already sold mining shares in the Moon.'

They all laughed nervously. Maybe it wasn't a joke.

⤻

'Is the UN worried the Wasted community is getting too powerful? Those patents bring in millions. Wasted is becoming the most powerful state internationally, but maybe not for much longer.'

'So, instead of the UN, we'll have artificial intelligence running the place?'

'Humans take risks, but AI is based on scooped up data others have used.'

'At the moment. That could change. What do you think, Grace? You're the Queen of Digital.'

There was a sudden group feeling in the cabin as if they were tackling a problem together. The Wasted community were all worried. The shantyboat labs had offered hope. But things were going wrong now.

Grace commented, 'AI can only be systematic based on the data they've accumulated. So can only advise on past input. Creativity is intelligence having fun.'

'Can a bot have a sense of humour? Pan didn't.'

'Depends on its data. They might have skimmed a "jokes" file from funny books. Not impulsive. Can't imagine a bot as a stand-up comic ...'

They all talked at once as if Pan was the common threat uniting them.

'Let's just worry about NOW. I don't like the idea of a BOT accusing me or us of a crime.'

'Lex had the perfect alibi. He wasn't on board.'

'Shadow the watch-cat was here. And the security footage must have recorded something useful,' someone suggested.

'You can't accuse a cat of attempted murder.'

'I've got access to the footage,' Grace admitted. 'I didn't feel comfortable sending it to Lex this time.'

'Why not? Have you looked at it? Who was there?'

'Wei Wei deserves protecting. She's been trying to help all of us, and then this happens.'

Kit wondered what it was on the footage that Grace didn't want Lex to see.

I don't talk much, but I think a lot. When I wear that ring, Grace knows what I think. So sometimes I take it off. Like now.

Wei Wei respected what asylum seekers could do. She was one of us too. No more war, which has made refugees like me and my family. And forced me to fight on both sides at different times. I fought for my family, not my country, and now they are gone.

A perfect place could NEVER work. I don't want scientific stuff to sell. I just want my own land to grow my own crops, and never see guards, guns or any government again.

But here is better than there. So I'll stay. Just meals and somewhere to sleep. And shifts around the garbage patch. We're like FIFOs. Fly in, fly out crew, except we paddle in and out.

So many of us. We're seen as a problem to be moved, not as people. THEY don't want to offer visas because then we stay. Coastal communities think we'll spoil their tourist trade. They blacklist cafes that give us food and clean water.

Temporary refugees are a permanent problem. But it's just people like me.

At first, individuals feel sorry for those who lost homes and lives and families and want to help. This fades fast.

Here ... no police. Not even security. Wei Wei never thought we'd need it. Utopia was not going to have crime. Wei Wei thought climate changing was the BIG problem ... But Wei Wei got it wrong and realised it after Cal's death. Greed was the problem.

WASTED?

It wasn't safe to release experimental diatoms into the oceans. What if Cal's death was not a one-off? Did the diatoms exposure cause it? Has Wei Wei made things worse?

If she dies, will anyone else know how to finish her projects? Will they?

～

14

What Happened to Wei Wei?

They huddled, cramped, on the few benches in the comms cabin, while the screens behind flashed and instruments beeped. As they'd just been investigated by a United Nations employed bot, it was as if they needed to be together to support each other. But at least one of them wasn't telling the truth.

Who was involved? It must have been one of them. Isolated on a shantyboat in the middle of the ocean. Very Agatha Christie mystery-ish, except it was fact not fiction. Kit glanced around. No Messi. That was a relief. Didn't he care what had happened to Wei Wei? Was he feeling guilty? Or was he worried that he would be blamed in some way? Where was he? Had he secretly left the *Satellite Freddie* after the UN Zoom?

'What's next?' someone asked.

But then, Messi appeared in the doorway, his shaggy hair looking more biblical than like Father Christmas's. His clothes weren't from another century, just jeans and a blue t-shirt printed with 'God-like' in black lettering.

Was this t-shirt the only one in Messi's collection? Or did he claim divine links often, in different colours. His God version of fashionable.

'What are you all doing? Holding a wake for Wei Wei? Is there more news?'

'She ISN'T dead … just in a coma,' Bolour explained. 'She's been taken to the mainland.'

'I didn't hear a chopper.'

'Search and Rescue couldn't land on our deck. She was taken by Medivac speedboat. Didn't you hear that? Or when she was stretchered down the steps? Frederick organised it.'

'Faster then my dragon boat, I guess,' offered Messi. 'That's gone anyway. Back to the rent-a-boat place. Now what will happen about the patents if Wei Wei can't continue?'

'Wei Wei is more than YOUR cash flow,' was a mutter from the back.

Messi looked annoyed.

'The Wasted State deals with the Lichtenstein private bank, not secret Swiss accounts.'

'How does he know that?' A different voice from the back.

Confrontationally, Messi spluttered in defence, 'You can't blame me for injuries to Wei Wei or her being in a coma. Why would I want her to stop experimenting? I need the patent to go through on her reputation. Wasted can't trade and get paid until that happens. Why should I cut off the money supply? And Wei Wei encouraged me to inform religious groups of what we were doing here for refugees. We were going to discuss funding me for that. I was the spiritual recruiter.'

'Might be true.'

It seemed Messi saw Wei Wei only as a money earner, for him.

How did he get money out of the Wasted account? Steal it? Or did he have an agreement with Lex?

'Wei Wei may not be able to work again, especially the way she was researching on the diatoms project. That was pretty high-level stuff.'

Kit was unsure what was true. There was so much he didn't know. As the latest newcomer, he was just getting to understand life on the shantyboat. Mainly, he listened, watched and sketched. It was safer not to say too much, especially when his mum was around. Most people knew Messi wanted to get his hands on money somehow, but if Wei Wei started to retest and took ages, or decided to stop the whole program ... Messi would miss out. So it was in his interests for the program to go ahead and the patents to be issued.

'And then the patents traded,' Fredrick added.

Kit took a quick sideways look at Frederick. Really weird how his thoughts could be read, even by Frederick. Was it related to the Lingo Ringo? Couldn't be just coincidence.

Just then Shadow peered around the now open door,

walked haughtily across the cabin and jumped onto the bench. She purred loudly. Kit checked her out. The cat looked undressed. No body-cam collar. Where was it? With Grace? Or Lex by special delivery?

'Where's your collar, Shadow? Are you missing Wei Wei?'

'Could it have been an accident?' The Great Garbo had bitten her nails right down. The edges were blood-reddish. 'Could she have fallen over the cat? A freak accident? I mean who falls over a cat? You can't charge a cat with attempted murder. Or manslaughter.' Nervously, she pulled her long sleeves over her wrists. 'Mightn't be anyone's fault.'

She was squashed alongside Kit. He was caught between the two females who had loud views on most subjects. As if the volume had been turned up when a bystander disagreed.

Was the Great Garbo trying to help? Or was this out of fear that she might be next? Kit wondered.

'Are you scared?' he whispered. 'Personally?'

GG shook her head. 'We're all different kinds of refugees, a random sample,' she said. 'Like me.'

Bolour overheard.

'Not really. Wei Wei picked people, especially asylum seekers, for their skills ... to train climate repairers.'

The Great Garbo didn't look satisfied with that answer. By now, Kit realised GG's pretence to have an opposite or outrageous point of view was just to get attention. She relied on 'youth' and no-one wanting to be seen to criticise a 'media' celebrity who was so young. She had her legs curled up on the seat like a little girl. He was younger and he didn't play the 'difficult' young person all the time. Why should she?

'So why did Wei Wei pick me?'

'I ask myself that question too,' Bolour muttered.

'Everybody moves or leaves home at some time, so why aren't adolescents called refugees?'

Across the cabin, Bolour's hearing was acute. She heard every word GG spoke.

'Because they're not trying to get away from political or religious persecution. Or from war atrocities. They don't believe in God and have never joined a political party. They're just anti-parent, temporarily or for a decade or so.'

'Duh ...' The Great Garbo didn't look satisfied with that answer either.

'Quarrelling doesn't solve anything,' Messi said, standing up. 'I'm off to collect a package ...' And he left.

'Was that the package from the chopper drop addressed to Messi?' asked Theo.

'Do you know what was in it?'

'Only guessing.'

'What?'

'Something he didn't want to be stopped by Customs or Quarantine.'

'Have we got Customs here?'

'No. But the chopper would be checked before it left the mainland airfield.'

'So would it have been something illegal? To do with one of his scams?'

'Maybe. Something Grace the Digital Queen couldn't intercept. Or talk about.'

'Money?'

'To pay, without going via the internet where Grace can check any digital stuff.'

'Risky.'

'Let's chase after him and ask him.'

'Ask Messi?'

If that reading thoughts extension did work, then they might get the truth. Unless Messi was turned off and not wearing his ring.

'If Wei Wei chose people with special skills, how come Messi is here?'

'Invited himself. Put up a good case that he would contribute to the welfare of the community via his religious connection. He's difficult to move. Wei Wei was too busy organising other stuff to make him leave.'

'Just don't make him Minister for Finance, or all the funds will be sent to his personal bank account.' Everyone laughed nervously.

'Has he really got a secret Swiss bank account?'

'Not secret if others know about it. He says the Wasted account is in Lichtenstein.'

'Just the key code is secret?'

'Messi says he came here to save us all.'

'The only thing he has saved is other people's money for himself. The Wasted community is possible cash flow for him. Even though we don't have money on the shantyboat,' explained Theo. 'Like on the Antarctic bases. No ATMs either.'

Steffi rarely gave Kit pocket money, and in the short time he'd been on board, he hadn't noticed that *Satellite Freddie* and all of the Wasted community was cash free.

Wasted was a strange mixture of off-grid 'making do' with recycling by old-timers like Frederick and hi-tech comms with Grace the Digital Queen, especially the Lingo Ringo.

Internationally they could Zoom link to the UN, but the dragon boat needed rowers in this soup of waste. Weird.

'WORK is the four-letter word not in Messi's vocabulary.'

'Messi is a religious nuisance. Hard to challenge him as he's always right.'

'And he shouts you down.'

The comms room emptied as people left to do their shift, because what else could they do? Or say? Until Wei Wei came out of the coma, if she ever did, they'd keep going.

Frederick and Kit cleaned up the galley, washing pans and drying mugs.

'Maybe you should follow the real leader of the Wasted community?'

'And who is that?'

'Guess.'

'Shadow?' suggested Kit, and they both laughed. 'Never catches a mouse, but has the lab rats under her control.'

⌐

Grace's skills were always in demand.

'You are so good with digital stuff, Grace. I want you to help me with something.'

'Again, Steffi?'

'I've heard about this zoo in Texas.'

'And get to the point, Steffi.'

'For a small fee, they will name a cockroach or rodent after your ex and feed it to one of the animals. San Antonio Zoo charges between $7 and $35 for this service and provides a digital greeting card, so the donor can let their former partner know how they really feel about them.'

'I don't do eco-revenge.'

'Thought you might say that. But it was worth a try. Thought I might talk about this online zoo service on my podcast.'

'Which ex?' Grace asked.

Kit overheard that. His dad wasn't just an ex.

'Is your new partner on board or back on the mainland?' Grace asked so politely, in a way that suggested she didn't believe Steffi.

'My soulmate is Rangi. His Māori name means sky. It feels like the right time to have a spirit guide. I have a BIG following.'

Kit had checked. She didn't.

'But I need new topics to talk about. I'm an online eco-influencer now.'

Mum talked about things she wanted to happen as if they had. It was SO embarrassing when your dad was still your dad and your mum was listed on dating apps. Photoshopped!

'Mum, does Rangi really exist?'

'In my mind he does.'

'At least he won't need a visa,' said Kit. 'If he's a spirit guide he won't have to go through immigration and get a passport stamped.'

Steffi laughed unexpectedly. 'No passport. ID photo. You're right, Kit. But I need a visa for you because you are my real family. And I had ex-boyfriends before I got married. I don't want revenge on your dad. He's a kind man.'

Kit smiled. True. But it was a relief to hear Steffi say that.

⌣

On the shantyboat, so many people seemed to answer Kit's thoughts when he hadn't even asked the questions aloud. He knew some of the seekers were super intelligent, but even so ... was it because of the Lingo Ringos they were wearing? Was there a hidden extension? He wanted to ask Grace more about her THOUGHTS answer to Pan.

She had said it was possible.

But Kit didn't get a chance to ask. Bolour got in first!

Bolour was hurrying ahead of him, not quite closing

the door behind her as she burst into Grace's cabin. So he waited outside. Their voices were quite loud. And Kit overheard enough.

'Grace, your Digital Lingo Ringo has taken my job as an interpreter … I appreciate all your work in developing it but … I'm worried about the hidden "THOUGHTS" function.'

'You've found it then?' Grace's voice was calm but Bolour sounded upset. 'Not yet. But I know it exists. Do you realise the WEAPON you've created, Grace?'

'Yes, I do.'

'As an interpreter, I'm diplomatic. I smooth out some of the answers. Imagine if foreign heads of government get the RAW thoughts of what their enemy REALLY thinks of them. No more jobs for diplomats. And dictators would have complete control.'

Grace's response was chilling. 'Not all have the THOUGHTS extension on their ring. I choose who gets it. They also need the ability to turn it on. It's a hidden extension. Optional. I know Mohammed has chosen to turn his off.'

'Is it a two-way function? Can an opponent's thoughts be understood without them reading yours?'

'Depends. Some malfunctions so far with blocking,' Grace admitted. 'That will be Mark 3.'

'Is it only you deciding who gets the extra extension?'

'So far.'

'Cross GG off your list. She says exactly what she thinks. A timebomb due to explode. Imagine if a leader could have vital secrets instantly transferred, unfiltered by interpreter diplomacy, during a crucial peace meeting.

'What about Messi? He's already negotiating with arms dealers, ocean mining oligarchs and bioterrorists. Or so he says.'

'Unsuccessfully so far and hopefully never. Messi doesn't have the hidden extension. At least not from me.'

'Could he have a pirated copy?'

'Maybe, but I'm sorting that now. Young Kit suspects that extra fact about the Ringo. He's an observant lad, and with that father, it's no surprise he's an original problem-solver. Others had given him a clue when they answered thoughts that he hadn't even spoken to them.'

'Will he act on that?' asked Bolour.

At first, Kit couldn't hear Grace's answer. So he moved closer. Eavesdropping was rude but how else could he understand what was going on?

'Grace, could I have the latest version? With the two-way function? Dual control so I'm in charge,' Bolour asked.

'Are you demanding or asking?' Grace replied.

'I need to know what's going on. I've been replaced as an interpreter. Now I need to decide my future. Will you give it to me, Grace?' Bolour insisted.

'Maybe it's already on your Ringo. You just haven't worked out how to use it. That is my safeguard.'

'You mean that a techie who works it out will have more

power than a compassionate leader trying to make wise decisions? Just another form of artificial intelligence?'

Grace's tone was serious. *'No. I'm only offering it to peacekeepers.'*

'And how long do you think that will work? You playing God.'

'Well, you want to be Head of State, don't you?'

Bolour shut the door firmly and pushed past Kit.

Kit had heard all of that. So he didn't think it was a good time to ask Grace anything more.

∽

Taking over a mid-ocean garbage patch that no-one wanted and recycling the plastic waste into a vital and saleable commodity other nations were eager to buy was a brilliant strategy.

Was someone jealous of Wei Wei?

And what about the cat-cam and collar? And where was Wei Wei's notebook?

Wei Wei was grumpy about interruptions, so if she often latched the door at night, that wasn't suspicious.

'Did she unlatch the door, let someone in and latch it again?' Kit asked Theo.

'If there was a second person, they'd have to latch the door from the outside as they left. Not possible,' Theo said. 'If she collapsed against the door, was it because someone attacked her? Or did she just trip? Or was she poisoned?'

Kit googled poisons, scientists and toxins.

'Historically, cover-ups have happened when scientists use little-known toxins to make murder look like an accident. That's what it says here.'

'And there was the arsenic poisoning case too. The lethal dose was administered to the scientist through a health drink he had consumed earlier,' Theo said.

Kit stopped googling. It wasn't helping. Who might know?

Theo looked thoughtful. 'There was that death after the anthrax postings in the United States. That scientist was one of the few people who would have been able to accurately trace exactly where the deadly substance had originated.'

'A scientist like Wei Wei? She's not going to poison herself!'

⌐

Quietly Kit climbed to the deck with access to Wei Wei's lab. Space was limited. It was hard to carry anything on these steps, especially another person. Frederick must have manoeuvred the unconscious Wei Wei on the stretcher with difficulty. Probably Theo helped. Maybe real paramedics were matched for height? In a real emergency you'd just be pleased to have any help, even if it was lopsided, as long as the patient didn't fall off.

Concentrate. Don't stray on ideas like equal-sized paramedics.

Kit needed to check the lab door before anyone asked him, 'What do you think you're doing?'

Which way did the sliding door work? Could you latch it only from the inside? Was Wei Wei alone in a lab latched from the inside, or was it not lockable?

Why hadn't he noticed earlier?

It was a sliding door. He switched on the light. There was a small catch on the inside of the door. He looked closely. It was broken. Recently? Of course, Frederick had jemmied it open. The marks were still there.

Did Wei Wei usually put the catch on the door when she was working alone? So she could concentrate? Or because she was scared?

Perhaps Steffi might know.

'Never noticed,' Kit's mum said.

Then he checked with Frederick.

'Was Shadow inside the lab, like ... when you ... carried ... like stretchered Wei Wei out?'

Frederick paused. 'I was concentrating on Wei Wei. Not the cat.'

'What about the kittens? Maybe they were back in the lab?'

Instant answer from the lab rat who liked small animals. 'No, the kittens weren't there,' he said. 'They're all still at the other end of the shantyboat, where I moved them out of Wei Wei's sight. Will organise a lift to the mainland for them soon. But every now and then, I take off Shadow's collar and put it around one of the kittens, to reassure them with her smell for a little while.'

'The door was hard to slide. Wei Wei had fallen against it, on the inside.' Frederick thought back to the moment. 'I had to force the door, so the catch was on the inside. Must go back and fix that sometime. Wasn't sure if this was a crime scene or not.'

Kit knew he shouldn't touch things if it was a crime scene, but there wasn't any of that yellow crime scene tape. Probably no-one on board had any. He was just trying to work out what happened.

Shadow was a useless witness.

Kit was sketching a mind map with Wei Wei in the middle. He drew faces on either side. Which ones wanted Wei Wei to stop the diatoms going into the ocean? And who wanted the money from the patents regardless of the effect on the rest of the world? The numbers were about even. But what about the ones he didn't know about?

And he wasn't even sure that Wei Wei's coma was due to an accident. Had she hit her head? Or had someone hit her? Or had fumes forced her to fall? Had she fallen over the cat? Could the Wasted project keep going if she wasn't here any more? Probably not. No-one else was skilled enough or enthused. Who else believed in retraining the other asylum seekers from political activists to climate repairers?

Bolour believed in utopia, sort of. Grace had the online skills.

Most refugees were unwilling to live on a garbage dump, so experimental labs on 'model satellite rafts' were just Stage 1. Not popular.

Mainly, they all needed Wei Wei's skills and drive. So why would anyone attack her?

15

Ring Superpower

'I'm sorry I lost the earlier ring, Grace. Does this new ring have a few … like … extra functions?'

'Ah. I wondered when you would ask me. Often digital devices have more capacity than the users realise.'

'Is it like … a spy ring?' Kit twisted the ring on his thumb, trying to get it off. 'How come it doesn't have a camera?'

'You've heard of taste testing? Well, this is ring testing. A private one for you, since you asked.' Grace put several rings on black velvet draped across the bench. Each ring gleamed. They were the same width and size. But the sparkling colours were slightly different. Greenish. Blueish. And a faint red.

'There's a part of your brain called the hippocampus. You store memories there. They can be translated by someone else wearing their ring on the same frequency as yours. That's why I issue my simplified version of the Lingo Ringo to some people and save the other version for special users. Occasionally I give it to those who will use it wisely,' Grace explained. 'This one is the simple ring.' She pointed.

'Which version did you give me?'

'Up to you to work that out.'

Kit colour-matched his ring. He looked closely at each of the others.

'The middle one.'

'With that ring on your finger, I can understand your thoughts, in any language. As long as I wear an equivalent ring.'

Kit pointed to the third ring on the velvet.

'So this ring has the highest superpower?'

Grace nodded. 'Slip it on your finger. Or your thumb.'

Kit wondered which one the Great Garbo had been given. But he just thought that, he didn't say it.

Grace smiled. 'The Great Garbo doesn't need the latest ring. But it would be very valuable for international heads of government negotiating peace or war. They'd pay anything for that immediate data. So would arms dealers.'

'It's sort of spying, isn't it? If only one side has it?'

'Have to trial the ring a bit more, sort out the glitches and finalise the patent.'

'That's really dangerous. What if BOTH sides have it? The same ring? It's like a weapon.'

'A bit like an arms race. But maybe they'll opt for peace instead of war. Use it as a deterrent. That's what Wei Wei hoped.'

'Useful for interviewing suspects. Or pinching others' ideas.'

'The hidden thoughts extension for politicians and strategists. Could charge anything for that.'

'The Digital Lingo Ringo with the thought translations extension would be useful for interviewing subjects in a murder mystery.'

'Only if the investigator knew about the thought extension. And had one.'

'So why are you telling me?'

Grace smiled. 'I'm sure you can work that out.'

Kit wasn't sure about that. But he'd try.

⁓

'My mum just wanted to ... like ... talk to the fish. You know she's into marine therapy.'

Frederick's laugh started at his mouth and went down his sinewy body. His droopy, 'lived-in' jeans had threadbare bits that were genuine holes, not fashion. His knee showed.

His skinny chest gasped and his Frederick tatt stood out on his arm.

'Marine therapy!' said Frederick. 'Don't understand half the fancy words they use around here. Especially the boffins. Easier when I was on my own. Much simpler than this now.'

'Frederick, when I got here and you explained about lab rats, I just thought you were good at working things out. Did you read my mind then? Or use the Lingo Ringo extension?'

'What do you think?'

Everybody on board seemed to be turning the questions back on Kit to answer for himself. Just like Dad used to do. It was so frustrating.

⤴

16

Palliative Care Hero

Dad's message was 'Come now.'

But Kit had a tough time getting to the Central Hospital, which had the Palliative Care Ward.

First, Kit had decided to take the *Sardine* to the mainland.

But when he checked deck-side, someone had borrowed his canoe again.

Since it was an emergency, he borrowed a kayak and left a note stuck on the deck near the mooring ring ...

WILL RETURN ASAP. KIT

Then, he wasn't even sure exactly which hospital entrance. But he used the GPS. Palliative Care was such a scary name for a hospital ward, but he followed the signs to the nursing desk.

'Could I see my dad please?'

Lying on a white hospital bed, his dad seemed to have shrunk. He had on a white hospital gown. The walls were white. He was lying very flat in the bed. The sheet was very white.

His face was faded as if he had gone in on himself. But he opened his eyes when Kit said, 'Dad, it's me, Kit.'

'You came?'

'Of course.'

Not the time to mention the missing *Sardine* canoe, or cycling into town on a borrowed bike.

Dad's breathing was very odd. Deep breaths and then almost nothing.

'I've got ... something ... for you, Kit. Look ... in the bedside drawer.'

Saying anything was an effort; it was as if he was casting around to capture the ideas and the words to connect them.

Kit pulled out pyjamas and other clothes in a plastic bag.

'Not those,' Dad said irritably. 'Plastic bag ... labelled "Kit", sealed tube.'

Dad was leaving out all the unnecessary words. Too much effort.

'This?'

'Yes. Take it.'

Dad's breath was laboured. A kindly nurse came into the room.

'We've made your dad as comfortable as possible. We took out some of the drips and tubes a little while ago.'

'Thank you.'

What did that mean? Was breathing on his own better or worse? The oxygen hissed. And there were so many electronic graphs flickering on the monitors. It was like an outer-space capsule linked up to the mother hospital ship.

'Hearing is the last sense to go. So talk to your dad, even if you're not sure he's listening.'

Kit didn't know what to say. He took his dad's hand, juggling the test tube with his other hand.

Dad struggled to press Kit's hand.

'Use it for yourself and anyone else you want to save. It's an antidote. Modified Lambda.'

Dad's face was strained and he closed his eyes. It was obviously an effort to collect his thoughts.

'Love you, Dad.'

Kit didn't know what else to do. He put the tube carefully in his pocket.

Then Dad spoke again, 'I'm so proud of you, Kit. Use your skills well.'

He closed his eyes before Kit could think of an answer.

This wasn't like a computer game with those sorts of choices. And then being able to replay the game. This was real. Artificial intelligence didn't do all-over-the-place emotions, like the way he felt now.

The kind nurse came into the room again.

'You might like to go out into the waiting room for a few minutes, while we make your father more comfortable. Your mother was here earlier and said she'd be back very soon, but your dad was waiting to see you.'

Why wasn't Steffi here now? Kit wouldn't ever be able to tell Dad about Wei Wei or about ANYTHING any more. Must be easier to believe in God and Heaven and all that stuff being taken care of for you. But Dad believed in scientific proof.

'I'll try, Dad,' Kit whispered as he left.

'Waiting Room' was a really bad name choice. Calming bluey-green landscapes, bland walls, hospital notices and boxes of tissues on the coffee table. Nobody would want to be there for this reason.

'I'm here,' Steffi spoke very quietly behind him. 'How's your dad at the moment?'

Kit didn't know what to say. 'When do you come here?'

'Recently? Every moment I can.'

Steffi paused and then filled up the awkward silence between them.

'Your dad kept his terminal diagnosis from me and I couldn't understand why he didn't want my help, even if we were divorced. I was stateless. It was almost as if I didn't exist. But months ago, Wei Wei passed on a message from the Red Cross that he was trying to find me. Around us, the country was at war, and the refugee camp was really a last resort. He asked for me to come and look after you.'

'To look after me?'

'Yes. So when Bolour and Wei Wei started the satellite labs, I joined them on the condition that you would be allowed to live there too. Rangi wasn't real, not like your father. He was just a spirit guide, so I felt there was someone to help me in my head during the tough times. When the military forces overran the ashram on the border, they destroyed my documents and I was sent to Camp 13.'

'I thought you didn't want me.'

'No, your dad needed you more.'

The nurse reappeared. 'Would you like to see your husband?'

'Are you okay, Kit, if I go in now?'

When Steffi left, Kit felt very alone.

But a surprise figure holding a block of chocolate and a scraggy bundle of supermarket flowers in crinkly paper appeared.

The Great Garbo was the last person Kit expected to see. She was nervously pushing up her woollen sleeves as if she was scared of his reaction to her being there. She nearly dropped the chocolate, but juggled the wrapped but squashed flowers to her other arm.

'So sorry about your dad. Frederick told me. So I came to sit with you. I'll go if you like. Have this.'

'What's with the chocolate?'

'It's good for shock. My parents used to say that. Here. Take it.'

'Er, thanks.'

Kit was numb. Usually he was wary of GG, unsure of what she'd say next. But now he was glad to see someone who was moving and real and alive. Her glowing skin looked so healthy. In hospitals, especially against the white bed linen, patients looked like drained shadows or had see-through skin, as Dad did.

'Theo asked me to give you some flowers. But he told me to choose them. He can't smell scents.'

'I know. He told me.'

'I'll find a vase or something and put them in water if you like. There were some jars in the alcove down the corridor. I'll borrow one.' GG left.

Kit sat stunned. Why did people send flowers? Weren't they for funerals? Too early. He didn't know what to do to help Dad now. Should he go back into the room? He couldn't make a decision. It was like living in a trance.

Footsteps. Two sets. Four feet.

The nurse came into the waiting room. She had her arm around Steffi, who looked weepy.

'So sorry, Kit. Your father has gone, Kit ... Passed away. Quickly and very peacefully. And he loved you so much.' Steffi gave Kit a hug.

'My condolences for your loss,' said the nurse.

She must have to say that a lot around here. But the nurse sounded genuine. As if she really cared for their family.

'Thanks.' That didn't seem the right thing to say for his dad's death. Thanks for death news, and his world would change. So final.

Kit put his arm around his mother. Everything was going to be very different now.

No more Dad to ask, or share things with.

GG arrived with the flowers stuffed in a weird glass container. The water sloshed inside.

She wasn't the best flower arranger in the world. But it didn't matter.

'Okay to cry. Sounded like your dad was a really good bloke.' Awkwardly GG put an arm around Kit's shoulder and patted his back. She had tears too.

'You'll be able to see him later, if you want to ... Or sit with him now.' The nurse tried to be comforting.

Kit wasn't sure about that. And the next hours and days were a blur. Time didn't matter.

But later, when they had a 'Celebration of Life' for Dad, rather than a funeral, he was so proud of all the positive things he learnt about his father. From strangers and former colleagues. Einstein, as they called him, stood up for his scientific findings, demanding proof. So Kit wasn't the only one who thought Dad was a hero.

Now Kit had to decide what to do with the legacy Dad left him. That was BIG!

⤳

With GG, Kit was leaning on the railing of the top deck, watching the waves. The ocean was SO big. How could one person, especially a teenager, make any difference?

'GG, you know that Law of the Sea 12-mile limit for legal stuff ...?'

'Yeah. Sort of.'

'Do you think it works for people?'

'Like, how?' The Great Garbo pushed up her stretched sleeves again. 'The 12-person limit? You can only make a difference that far? The people you see around you?'

Kit was still thinking. Easier to draw. And he had 12 shantyboat caricatures on his sketchpad already.

GG smiled. 'You're wrong, Kit. What about protesting in the street with banners? Hundreds follow me. That's more than 12 people.'

'No, YOU'RE wrong, GG.' Frederick came up behind them. 'Street protests just stuff up the traffic and annoy other people. They don't change afterwards. And still throw their plastic away.'

'Hunger strike?'

'Only hurts the one doing it. No point,' Frederick commented.

Kit was pleased to hear that.

'What's the biggest problem? What do you think, Kit? And what are you going to do about it? That's your dad's legacy. Asking the right questions. And then getting REAL answers.'

Kit felt the reassuring shape of Dad's antidote in his pocket. Which was the answer?

'Like my media interviews?' GG had been listening intently. 'Or podcasts like Steffi's?'

'Some of Steffi's passions go sideways but she has a good heart. Not sure how effective. But the emergency Cal tent is useful. That may turn out to be the best idea,' Frederick said. 'You can't fix a big problem, but you can work out the best ways to use your energy. You only have minutes in your life and you can stuff around or do one tiny thing each day. And move in the direction of improving things.' Frederick adjusted the water recycling that covered the upright seedlings, with the solar panel on top. 'Not all these seeds will grow, but a few will.'

Frederick continued, 'Look at Mohammed. He's had really bad things happen in his life. But he knows Wei Wei was trying to solve the plastic pollution problem and get visas for the refugees. He can't think of any other way to help. So he does another shift around the garbage patch. A tiny difference. Better to build something than destroy.'

'What?' asked Kit.

Frederick shrugged. 'Have to find some little thing that you can do that helps the big picture. And doesn't make things worse. Don't do it just for ego.'

'Big picture' gave Kit the idea.

'That's what Einstein left you as a legacy. Ability to question.'

'I can draw. But I can't see how that helps.'

'It could.'

'You mean like Wei Wei and her testing that takes so long? And it seems wasted, but ... the lab rats will continue?'

'Yes. Or your dad, Einstein. He used his time well but his views were a bit ahead of the others so they cried him down.'

'What's the difference between Messi and the seekers?'

Frederick's expression changed. 'Messi only does things for himself to get money and power.'

'Yeah,' said GG. 'He's not the only one.'

'We all get it wrong sometimes. Accidents happen, like to Wei Wei, but then others step in and carry on.'

Kit decided to ask, 'Do you think plastic pollution in the ocean is the biggest problem at present?'

Frederick looked thoughtful. 'No. But it's the one to tackle now.'

Kit doodled, designing a stamp of the Great Garbage Patch.

'What's that?' asked GG, pointing to the word 'Utapia?' at the bottom of the stamp.

'Spelled it wrong,' Frederick said.

'Utopia is a place where things work perfectly,' Kit said defensively.

'Dystopia is the reality,' said Frederick. 'Things don't always work out.'

GG gave a tiny smile. 'This place or the stamp?'

'Everybody gets things wrong at times,' said Frederick. 'Just have to keep trying.'

⌐

17

Expo: Refugee Legal Aid Cartoon Kit

The tiny jellyfish with sneakers was his squiggled signature on the bottom of each exhibit. A surge of emotion grew like a tide within him.

The webcam zoomed in. Kit was still on *Satellite Freddie* and his sketches had travelled further than him. To New York. So cool. He was thrilled at the camera eye view of his work exhibited in the United Nations building. He could even read the sign in the background.

Surprisingly, the exhibition idea had been supported by GG. He always called her GG now because the Great Garbo was such a mouthful to pronounce. He wouldn't say they were friends yet, just getting along better since she had turned up at Palliative Care and been supportive about his dad when Kit felt so alone.

Then she suggested to Lex that having an exhibition of Kit's sketches would help the Wasted brand.

'Not interested,' said Lex.

Earlier, Kit suspected Lex had something to do with the drone that illegally pirated data about Grace's latest ring with the hidden thoughts extension.

Kit joined the Zoom and mentioned the drone.

'What do you know about the theft by drone?' Lex asked on screen.

'Grace may have built in a once-only usage,' suggested Kit. 'On the latest ring. Impossible to copy. If it were sold on, the customer would be furious.'

There was silence on screen.

'I'll get back to you,' Lex switched off.

'Is that true?' GG asked. 'About Grace's latest ring?'

Kit shrugged. 'Check with Grace.'

Next day, Lex agreed to organise the exhibition. And donate all profits. And return the ring. Kit wasn't sure if Dad would have agreed on how Kit did this, but he would have agreed on why.

The UN Gallery was SO long. The cathedral walls went right up to the stained glass roof with the wooden beams. Those very important people, the VIPs, couldn't get to their meetings until they walked along these corridors and they couldn't avoid seeing Expo: Refugee Legal Aid sketches by Kit all the way along the walls. Even if Kit's signature was an unreadable squiggle with a tiny jellyfish in sneakers at the bottom. He'd asked for sneaker footprints to be made on the floor walking to each exhibit, but Lex said, 'No, not in the budget.'

'Wasted Refugees' was added by Lex under each enlarged sketch. With an 'about the subject' bio. And dot points about how Wei Wei's bioremediation patents were used to reclaim land. And the website for further details for investors. And how the garbage patch had been recycled as a digital visa-issuing state. Asylum seekers were doing it for themselves. Strategic climate repair.

When she looked at his second-try lizard sketch of her, after he tweaked it, GG had been pleased. Kit expected her to be annoyed. Instead of seeing a show-off, she liked the vivid colours of the frilled-neck lizard. She was flattered that someone drew her. Different from being photographed for social media. Or taking selfies from odd angles.

'So colourful,' GG said. 'Let me see the others.'

'Frederick as the dried mackerel is the best fit. Lex the lawyer is definitely a wild dog.' She laughed. 'Lex is just part of the funding industry. Good at creating paid work for himself.'

Kit had only met Lex via screen and thought he was like a wild dog with an acute sense of smell for opportunities. He was sniffing out how the Wasted patents could be best protected, so that he would get his share of commissions. But Kit couldn't say that to Lex, so he made him into a cartoon wild dog with a sniffy nose.

When he first started sketching, Kit did it just for himself.

He showed what he saw. Now he was nervous. Would others be insulted? A caricature was a bit exaggerated and meant to be funny. And in bad times, humour helped. He really missed Dad, who would have loved these sketches. But the stamp hadn't worked so well.

'Wei Wei is my favourite sketch. Sort of scavenger bird. Intelligent elf owl who feeds on insects.'

'Sort of recycling from the garbage patch. Wei Wei did that. You're right, Kit.'

GG had changed. More helpful. Less prickly. Kit didn't understand why. Was it because she was no longer Head of State? Not pretending any more? She was still keen on climate repair, but ... Wei Wei's continuing coma had made a difference to all of them. They had to act for themselves now.

The camera panned down the corridors as if working through a maze.

Visitors could start anywhere and visit the sketches in any order.

'Symbolic. Refugees have so many dead ends and detours. Start anywhere.'

On a table at the back door were piles of the Refugee Legal Aid Comic Books.

'Help Yourself' said the sign in most languages. 'Free.'

What would the people from the Wasted community think? Had he been too honest? Kit hadn't meant to be unkind.

WASTED?

He just drew people as he saw them in the form of animals, insects and marine creatures.

His sketches were like a cartoon kit ... a sort of choose-your-own-path to get a visa, with diagrams and not many words, except in speech balloons.

Kit had used his original caricatures of Wasted asylum seekers to explain in pictures what refugees needed to do to reach safety or get a visa or start afresh in a new world.

'Got a bit of an idea for those who can't read ... the refugees who can't read English or their own language. Might help with their legal stuff. Here ...'

'Comic graphics?' queried Theo.

'Digital too?' queried Grace. 'Possibilities.'

'Wei Wei's sketch should go first. Wasted was her idea.'

'No, it was Bolour, when they were in Camp 13.'

'Was it?'

'If it's a corridor of sketches ... along the passageway, they're equally important.'

That slim, expensively suited man with a necklace above his designer t-shirt and a Lex name tag stood in front of Kit's artwork. The lawyer wasn't happy with Kit's caricature of him.

A visitor heading for a meeting commented, 'Wild dog with acute sense of smell. Is that you?'

GG laughed but luckily they were on mute on *Satellite Freddie*. Lex couldn't hear them. But they could hear him.

Lex 'owned' the project in public, so he had to speak in

favour. 'Had qualms about the Wasted community as my clients at first. But now, financially, brand Wasted are serious players. They could end up running our world and controlling all resources, so I want to remain involved. And with Wei Wei unable to continue ...'

Lex turned off the Zoom.

〜

I suffer from allergies. That was my excuse to Wei Wei. No way was I visiting the garbage patch site in person. Sorted that at the start of our relationship. But the financial possibilities convinced me to get involved at a distance. Trading biowaste patents based on seeker research guided by Wei Wei was lucrative. She wanted the visas for the refugees and money to sponsor their families, the ones who had survived. I was more interested in the legal percentages as my fees. Legal advice in chargeable minutes, plus bonuses.

Biofuel was the first patent. Unbelievably successful. But only possible with the Wasted community becoming a legal state. They needed my advice on that.

Others have tried water-reclaimed territories, but Wasted did it better from garbage patch recycling and labs on satellite shantyboats. They have hit on a brilliant solution. Geographic borders are outdated by digital. I am their lawyer and I'll help them patent every climate repair idea. In my best interest too, of course. I'm excellent on contract clauses.

I didn't always understand the science, but I knew how to sell a bio-idea to needy nations.

I'll know as soon as the lab rats discover anything significant. Start the patent process immediately even if they want more trials to make sure it's safe. Wei Wei saw the bio-recycling as a means to help refugees, but she was so ethical and wouldn't go ahead unless things were safe.

After Cal's death, Wei Wei didn't want to patent anything without spending months retesting. We didn't have the time. I needed to know as soon as she found something new. Chances were she wouldn't tell me. So Shadow's body-cam was my insurance. Grace collected the footage for me. And Grace scanned Wei Wei's notebook as proof of original concept for my legal files, just in case. The actual notebook was lost. Must be on the shantyboat somewhere. Using the drone for pirated data to circumvent Grace was a mistake. The one I delegated the job to had no idea what was being carried. But the ring had patent possibilities if Wei Wei's health was still doubtful.

There was a risk that if we released the diatoms in the ocean, others would be affected like Cal. I had contracts lined up with internationals, so we needed Wei Wei's results NOW. But she was determined to keep retesting. The lab rats are waiting on Wei Wei's recovery.

When I'm asked, 'What is your specialty as a lawyer?' 'Refugees' is my answer. Patents from asylum seekers who have become climate problem-solvers is my reality. I'm part of the new refugee industry.

Where are the borders? Are geographic borders outdated, with wars, digital maps and man-made islands?

The law of a country only extends a certain distance into the sea. International trading interests me more. Especially ocean floor mining licences. Then there's the question of merchandising – merch based on garbage rafts, t-shirts, water bottles, Steffi's better recycling ideas, like the Cal tent ...

And, of course, with Wei Wei in a long-term coma, I've organised Power of Attorney and can sign all legal documents on her behalf.

〜

'Have a look at this. It's the footage we watched from Wei Wei's lab.'

'The body-cam from Shadow's collar?' GG asked.

Kit nodded. 'Some parts are really dark, like maybe they could have been wiped.'

'Didn't the lab rat take the collar off Shadow so the kittens had a familiar smell? So, there's no way we can track everything that happened in Wei Wei's lab that night.'

'No. But maybe it was an accident. Maybe someone was protecting Wei Wei.'

Had the lab rat taken the cat-cam to protect Wei Wei? Not just to calm down the kittens? Or had Grace?

What didn't they want Lex to see? And where was the notebook?

Kit wondered if Dad would have approved of what his son was doing now. Kit would have loved him to be here, but maybe he was, in spirit. Not like Mum's Rangi.

Time to face Lex.

On request, Lex agreed to a face-to-face call. There were cartoons on his desk, Kit noticed.

'Let's move on. This UN exhibition is important to help promote the Wasted patents internationally. It's really a trade exhibition,' Lex said, sorting the papers.

'Is it? I thought it was a way of helping refugees.'

'That too.' Lex showed Kit. 'Now if you digitally autograph these first editions of the Refugee Legal Aid Cartoon Kit, I'll be able to arrange for them to be auctioned.'

'Auctioned? But these are free for any refugee. I donated them.'

Lex paused. 'Not a good idea for us, financially.'

'Us?'

'In memory of Cal and a tribute to Wei Wei.'

'Yes. But all the money must go to the refugee fund,' Kit insisted.

For the second time, Lex lost.

⌐

'I've brought you a snack. Unburnt toastie.'

'Theo didn't make it then?'

Now when GG and Kit ended up eating together between shifts, they used old-fashioned questions, rather than turning rings to the thought translation frequency and tuning in. It was more fun to guess what the other thought.

'Thanks for helping me with the Expo. What are you doing next, GG? Looking after animals? Might be safer. They don't talk back, they're loyal and they love you whatever you do.'

'Not all animals. What about Shadow?'

Kit took a big bite of his toastie and the cheese oozed out. He chewed thoughtfully.

'Steffi told me about karma. About how Dad and Wei Wei did good stuff and were respected later, even if they had things go wrong in between. Do you believe in karma?'

'You mean when bad things happen to you, it's a payback?'

'No. More like, that you get what you deserve. Good people get good things. Bad people get bad. Like Messi has to pay back any money he took. Did you hear Wei Wei is out of her coma, but she's pretty weak still. Frederick told me. That's good news.'

'Awesome.' GG looked a bit weepy. As if she really cared.

'Wei Wei may not be able to finish her testing. But the lab rats will.'

'Do they know what happened to her?'

'Not sure. It might have been Shadow's fault. If she tripped her and she fell hard. But there's no record of what happened because the collar cam was with the kittens.'

'Pan won't be able to interview Shadow.' GG smiled. 'Cats don't do AI.'

'You haven't any proof of that. They might be on a digital wavelength we don't know.'

They both smiled.

'Kit, I found this.' Mohammed held out Wei Wei's notebook.

'On the top shelf in the lab?' Kit recognised the type of notebook.

'No. In the secret lab drawer,' Mohammed said.

Kit skimmed it. 'Proof of all her tests. D'you think Grace scanned it, to keep Lex under control?'

GG shrugged. 'They think Wei Wei fell over the cat. So Frederick thinks I should look after Shadow. If I look after her, is that karma?'

Kit laughed. 'For you or for the cat?'

Now Kit had to think of how to pass on Dad's legacy, which was more than Lambda in a test tube. The modified Lambda could neutralise and protect from what had killed Cal, but ...

⌒

Acknowledgements

Thanks for the advice from Australian Antarctic expeditioners Peter Cheers and Garry Mayo, physicist Dr Zoltan Kerestes, Dr Miki Pohl, and infectious diseases physician Dr David Sheffield. A special thanks to Kim Edwards, cover designer Joh Fitzpatrick, editor Dalida Boustead, and my test readers of varied ages.

www.ingramcontent.com/pod-product-compliance
Lightning Source LLC
Chambersburg PA
CBHW050020070726
47506CB00015B/624